THE GHOST OF EMMA LOUISE

THE GHOST OF EMMA LOUISE

MARY LYLE READ

Illustrated by Ingrid Koepcke

Abingdon / Nashville

The Ghost of Emma Louise

Library of Congress Catalog Card No.: 79-3686

READ
 The ghost of emma louise.
 TN: Abingdon Press
 8003   791018

ISBN 0-687-14218-0

Manufactured in the United States of America

For my sister
Ruth Virginia Lyle

I

Emma Louise Jones did not believe in ghosts. She was nine years old, and she knew a thing or two. She knew ghosts are make-believe creatures in stories, although they sometimes seem very real indeed. Late, late at night, when the lights are out and the grownups asleep, and the moon is making shivery shadows in corners of the room and someone starts telling ghost stories, you can feel as if a ghost is there in the shadows waiting to reach out and touch you. Of course, it is only your imagination. Or is it?

Emma Louise Jones was a half orphan. Her father was dead, and she lived with her mother in a very old wooden house on the edge of Lewisville. The house had once been white, but dirt and time had turned it gray and made it look old and tired. Now it sagged in places making cracks through which the wind whistled in the winter. Emma Louise's mother would listen to the wind whistling around the house, and she would say, "Oh, dear, we must do something about this poor old house." But nothing was ever done for Emma Louise and her mother were poor.

They had enough to eat. After that there wasn't much money left for anything else. They got along quite nicely, however, until one cold winter when the price of everything went up. "Inflation," Mrs. Jones called it, and said they would have to tighten their belts and turn down the heat because food and fuel cost so much.

Mrs. Jones shopped for bargains; they ate a lot of beans, and they turned the heater way down. The house was not too uncomfortable until one blustery night when the wind kept pushing cold air through the cracks. Mrs. Jones put a blue sweater over her red sweater, and Emma Louise put her green sweater over her yellow one, but still they were cold.

"We can't turn the heater up," Mrs. Jones said. "I haven't paid last month's fuel bill yet, but I will put your grandfather's old army blanket on my bed tonight, and I will let you have the Quilt. I'll get it from the trunk in the attic right now."

When Emma Louise got back to her room from brushing her teeth, there spread out on her bed was a beautiful patchwork quilt. Mrs. Jones, tucking it in, said to Emma Louise, "You must be very, very careful with the Quilt. It was made by your great-great-grandmother."

Emma Louise hopped quickly into bed and sat up studying the Quilt. She had never seen anything like it. Tiny pieces of fabric of different kinds and colors were sewn together to form beautiful designs. Words were embroidered in the four corners of the Quilt and at the top and the bottom. Emma Louise read them out loud. "Faith, Hope, Charity, Felicity, Patience, and Prudence. Why are they written on this Quilt?" she asked.

"Those are the names of your great-great-grandmother's children," her Mother answered. "She had six girls, and this Quilt was made from pieces of the dresses they wore when they were growing up. Faith, Hope, Charity, and Felicity's dresses make up the four corners. Patience and Prudence's dresses are the center panel."

"She cut up their dresses to make the Quilt?" Emma Louise asked.

"Oh, no," her mother replied. "She used the scraps left over when the dresses were made. People didn't buy dresses in stores then as they do now. She would never have used worn fabric for such a magnificent quilt as this. It is a real treasure, and you must be very careful of it. You must never eat or color in bed when you are using it."

Emma Louise nodded her head and snuggled

down under the cozy covers. She listened to the wind shake the old house, and, feeling very snug and warm, she soon fell asleep.

During the night she dreamed a little woman dressed in old-fashioned clothes was rocking in a big chair in the corner of her room. That was all—only the woman silently rocking. The next morning when Emma Louise woke up, she almost forgot the dream.

That night when Emma Louise went to bed the wind was not howling, the room was not as cold as the North Pole, and she was not sleepy. She was hungry, for she had not eaten much supper. She never did when they had fish. Thinking longingly of a peanut butter and jelly sandwich, she scooted to the kitchen and made a thick gooey one. At the kitchen table, the floor was cold to her bare feet. She thought of the cozy bed upstairs. She remembered her mother's warning about eating in bed, but she decided she would be careful and not dribble.

She woke the next morning to find her mother standing by her bed, a grim look on her face. "Emma Louise, Emma Louise, I told you not to eat in bed. You have ruined the Quilt. It has never had such spots in all its hundred years." She sounded as if she were about to cry.

There on the quilt were bread crumbs, but worse than that there were gooshy globs of peanut butter and jelly. "I'm sorry, Mother," Emma Louise said, and meant it.

But her mother hardly heard her. "I have no choice but to take it off your bed," she said. "Sleeping cold will be punishment enough for you. If I work very carefully," she continued almost as if to herself, "Perhaps, I can get the spots out. Then it will be back to the attic for the Quilt. It is our only heirloom."

——II——

That night WAS cold. Emma Louise put on two night gowns, a pair of knee socks, and her bathrobe, but she still felt chilly. She curled up in a round shivery ball and tried to sleep. Toward morning she began to feel quite comfortable and not cold anymore, but she was too sleepy to wonder why. She just stretched out of the cramped ball she had been in and enjoyed the warmth. While she slept she again dreamed about the small woman silently rocking in the corner of the room.

The next morning she was awakened by her mother shaking her and saying, "Emma Louise, Emma Louise."

"Oh, dear, what have I done now?" Emma Louise asked sleepily.

"Young lady, you know very well what you've done," her mother answered. "You sneaked up to

12

the attic last night for the Quilt and put it on your bed."

Emma Louise sat up quickly. There spread about her was the Quilt. That was why she had been so warm.

"I didn't do it," she protested.

"Now, Emma Louise," her mother said sternly, "Don't add fibbing to disobedience. I didn't put the Quilt on your bed, and it couldn't get here by itself. But how you found the trunk in that dark attic I don't know."

Emma Louise didn't know either. She wondered if she could have walked in her sleep. It was a scary thought.

Her mother smoothed the Quilt with loving fingers. "It was cold last night," she said. "I should not have taken the Quilt from you. I will allow you to keep it on your bed, but you must promise never to eat in bed again. We have a responsibility for this beautiful family heirloom."

"I promise, I promise," Emma Louise said quickly, and she meant it.

The Quilt stayed on Emma Louise's bed. Each night she was warm and comfortable, and each night she had the same dream about the woman rocking silently near her bed. She started to tell her mother one morning. Just as she had said, "Mom, I've been having the craziest dream," her mother looked at the clock and said "Emma

Louise, you are as slow as molasses in January. Finish your breakfast, brush your teeth, and run along, or you will be late for school." So Emma Louise didn't tell her mother anything about her dream.

That night the woman of her dream spoke to her. But the strange thing was that this time Emma Louise was quite sure she was not asleep and dreaming. She was still sitting up in bed. The woman in the chair in the corner of the room spoke again. "Child, what is your name? Speak up, speak up. Has the cat got your tongue?"

Emma Louise just sat and stared. She wasn't exactly scared for the woman had a kindly expression. But it was a while before she finally managed to say, "I'm Emma Louise, Emma Louise Jones, but who are you?"

"Emma Louise, Emma Louise," the woman repeated. She seemed pleased. "At last they had the good sense to name one for me." She looked closely at Emma Louise, then nodded her head approvingly. "You seem to be a child with some gumption. I do believe we will get along very well."

Emma Louise, still sitting up in her bed, didn't feel the chill in the room at all. The little woman didn't seem to either although her long, tight-waisted dress was not heavy, and she wore no wrap. Emma Louise still stared fascinated.

14

"Haven't they taught you it's rude to stare?" the little woman demanded sharply.

"Why, yes," Emma Louise admitted, still staring. "It's that I don't know who you are or what you're doing in my room."

The woman seemed quite annoyed. "Haven't they taught you anything?" she asked. "Haven't they shown you the family pictures? One of me was quite good. I was one of Mr. Phipps' first customers when he opened his photographic studio, the one on State Street."

Emma Louise shook her head. She had seen no family pictures, and she had never heard of Mr. Phipps and his photographic studio.

"That is a shame," the woman sighed. "It's a good thing I'm here now to take over some of your upbringing." She paused for a moment wrinkling her brow. "I'll have to figure out how you fit on the family tree," she said. "What is your mother's first name?"

"Penelope," Emma Louise answered.

"Of course," the woman beamed happily. "Gertrude's child, who was Felicity's child."

"Don't you see?" the little old woman said impatiently, as Emma Louise looked more puzzled than ever. "It's as plain as the nose on your face. You are Penelope's child; Penelope was Gertrude's child; Gertrude was Felicity's child; and Felicity was my child. Now do you know who I am?"

16

Emma Louise shook her head.

"Why I am your great-great-grandmother," the old woman said. "I made that quilt, and I brought it down from the attic the night you lay there shivering in your sleep."

Emma Louise's head was spinning.

"So they named you Emma Louise." Her great-great-grandmother smiled at her. "Took them long enough to name one for me. Not only are you my great-great-grandchild, you are my namesake."

"But," Emma Louise stammered. "You can't be my great-great-grandmother. She's dead. Even my grandmother is dead."

"You're absolutely right," the woman agreed. "I am dead. Whatever gave you the notion I wasn't?"

"Well," Emma Louise stammered, "You're sitting here talking to me."

The little old woman leaned forward. "Haven't you ever heard of a spirit?" she asked.

"A spirit?" Emma Louise looked puzzled.

"Spirit, spirit," the woman repeated somewhat waspishly. "Ghost, if you like. Myself, I prefer spirit. It's more proper and descriptive."

"Of course I've heard of ghosts." Emma Louise replied. "Who hasn't heard of ghosts, but I don't believe in them. Everyone of any intelligence knows they don't exist. They're make-believe things in stories."

17

"I'm not in a story," the woman snapped. "I'm living proof that you are wrong about that."

"But you're not living," Emma Louise answered. "You're dead. You said so yourself."

"Yes, yes, of course," the woman agreed. "That was a figure of speech. A poor choice of words. I meant my talking to you here is proof that I exist, call me whatever you like."

"Oh, you do certainly seem to be here," Emma Louise said after a moment, "But maybe I'm just imagining you. Mom says I have a vivid imagination."

"Imagination, indeed," the woman snorted. "How could a child like you possibly imagine someone like me? Why you didn't even know my name. Why, you hardly knew your grandmother's name. And you didn't know what I looked like."

"That's just it," Emma Louise answered. "I don't know any of that. How do I know I'm not imagining the way you look? I have no proof that you look like my great-great-grandmother."

"Proof, proof." The woman seemed ready to explode. "You are a most irritating child." Then she calmed down and smiled at Emma Louise. "Come to think of it, child, that was an intelligent question. Shows you are not easily taken in. Shows you are like me in more than name. I was never easily taken in either. I knew what she had in mind right from the start."

"What who had in mind?"

The old woman waved Emma Louise's question aside. "Never mind that now," she said. "First things first, and first of all I must show you that I am who I say I am. I must give you proof. Come with me."

With that she got up and walked through the closed door. Emma Louise just stared. She was sure now she was dreaming. In moments the woman walked back into the room through the closed door. "Come, come, child," she commanded impatiently. "Make haste. Follow me." This time Emma Louise followed, after opening the door.

The hallway was dark except for moonlight shining through the window. The narrow, creaky attic stairs seemed to end in pitch blackness. In fact, Emma Louise could only see the first two steps clearly. As she somewhat reluctantly followed the woman up the stairs, she realized that she could see quite well. It was as if the woman herself were a light showing the way.

At the top of the stairs the woman drifted through the closed attic door leaving Emma Louise in darkness. but she quickly glided back through the door, making it possible for Emma Louise to find the doorknob.

"I'm sorry I left you out there in the dark, child," the woman apologized. "I keep forgetting how it is for you ordinary people, having to open doors and such. Really quite a nuisance."

In the attic the woman led Emma Louise to an old trunk. "Open it, child," she commanded. Emma Louise obeyed, and the odor of mothballs filled the air. The trunk was full of old clothes, papers, and faded photographs. In one of the photographs Emma Louise saw the likeness of the woman.

"You see, you see," chortled the woman. "That's my picture, my photograph, the one I had made in Mr. Phipps' studio down on State Street. Now do you believe you are not imagining me?"

Emma Louise knelt by the trunk in stunned silence. She didn't know what to believe.

"My, you are a doubting Thomas," the woman said impatiently. "Turn the picture over. Read what it says on the back."

There in a spidery hand was written, "Emma Louise Atkins." The woman beamed with satisfaction. "Now do you believe I am who I say I am?"

Emma Louise nodded numbly. "Yes, yes—I do, and—and that means I believe in ghosts." And although she felt a tickly shiver run down her spine, she was not in the least frightened of the little woman.

"Good," said the woman briskly. "Now that that is taken care of we must be about the business I am here for. Close the trunk. Mind you don't catch me in there. I've had enough of that. By staying too close to my Quilt, I must have been locked in that trunk three or four times over the last hundred years. Last time your grandmother locked me in was when your mother was a tiny girl. Believe me it's more cramped than the tomb. Humiliating too. Imagine me, Emma Louise Atkins, born Emma Louise Lewis, being caught off guard like that. I've been in there so long I even smell like the trunk. Haven't you noticed the odor of mothballs about me?" Emma Louise realized that she had, but she had thought the smell came from the Quilt.

"I was certainly relieved when your mother came for the Quilt," the woman continued. "Believe me, I hopped right out of there."

"She didn't see you?" asked Emma Louise.

"Of course not," the woman answered. "Nobody sees me unless I want them to. Sometimes they don't even see me when I want them to. Really I've had quite a hard time appearing to people over the years. It's most aggravating. People seem to have developed a complete blind spot where ghosts are concerned." She beamed at Emma Louise. "That's why it's so gratifying to find someone at last who has an eye for ghosts." Suddenly her smile turned to a frown, and she said, "Don't you know the first thing about ghosts or spirits? Don't you know they only appear when they want to appear?"

Emma Louise, getting a bit miffed at being put down, answered tartly, "I know one thing. Ghosts go through things like closed doors. You just did. How come you couldn't get out of a trunk?"

"Oh, child," the woman smiled approvingly, "you really are like me in more than name. You've got a head on your shoulders. That's a logical question, and the answer is simple. I was cramped in a little knot and couldn't get any momentum. To go through things you have to be standing and free. Do you understand?"

Emma Louise nodded, although she wasn't quite sure what "momentum" meant.

Her great-great-grandmother seemed satisfied. "Good," she said. "Now let's get back to your room. It's so drafty up here, it nearly wafts me away."

Back in her room, Emma Louise jumped into her bed. She did not lie down, but she pulled the Quilt up around her shoulders. She had gotten so cold in the attic that she was shivering, and her teeth were chattering. "Child," the woman clucked sympathetically, "Before you go back to bed you need to have a good fire built in that fireplace to warm this room."

"Oh, no," Emma Louise answered quickly. "That fireplace hasn't been used in years. Mom says a fire in there would burn the house down.

The house is cold because the heater is turned down."

"Then make haste and turn it up."

"I can't do that. Mom says we haven't paid last month's fuel bill yet. You see," she added, "we're poor."

"I can well believe that," the woman said, looking around the room critically. "My fine things seem to be gone. 'The sins of the fathers are visited upon the children unto the third and fourth generations,' " she added softly.

Emma Louise hadn't the faintest notion what she meant and watched the silent woman rock faster and faster until it seemed she would surely turn the chair over. Suddenly she stopped and said, "Oh, that woman, that deceitful woman."

Emma Louise waited till the woman had calmed down a bit, and then she asked the question that had puzzled her.

"Great-great-grandmother," she began, "if you couldn't get out of the trunk because you didn't have momentum—" she paused a moment, "how did you get out of your grave?"

The woman was lost in thought and didn't answer.

Emma Louise asked again, "Gamma, how did you get out of your coffin if you couldn't get out of the trunk?"

The woman stopped rocking immediately and

glared at Emma Louise. "Young lady," she said, "Just how did you address me?"

"Gamma," Emma Louise said. "It's short for great-great-grandmother. That is much too long to say."

The old woman thought for a moment, then said, "Perhaps you are right. Still it does seem somewhat disrespectful." She rocked silently, then said, "Nevertheless, I shall allow it. You may call me Gamma."

"Thank you, Gamma," Emma Louise answered. "But you still haven't told me."

"Told you what?" Gamma asked.

"How you got out of your coffin if you couldn't get out of a trunk."

"Child," Gamma beamed at her, "that is another good question, but the answer is simple, too. I didn't get out, because I never got in. I made quite sure of that. I wanted to stay around and take care of a few things I didn't have time to attend to before my untimely death." She added almost as if to herself, "I knew which direction the wind was blowing. I knew what would come about. I knew what was in that deceitful woman's mind."

The clock in the old courthouse began striking the hour. They both counted. It was midnight.

"Gracious sakes alive," Gamma said. "Child, I must be on my way. I've kept you up much too long. You'll dawdle in school tomorrow. While you get your sleep, I'll whisk off and tend to a few things. There's much to do".

"No, no," Emma Louise protested, but the woman and the rocker vanished.

So excited she could not sleep, Emma Louise lay under the cozy covers and puzzled over what she had seen and heard. What did Gamma mean, "There's much to do?" Who was the deceitful woman? What had she been up to? Emma Louise could hardly wait to tell her mother about the family ghost.

——III——

But the next morning a strange thing happened as Emma Louise sat staring at her oatmeal. She began to feel that the events of the night before had never really happened. Something as ordinary as oatmeal can make something as extra-ordinary as a ghost seem unbelievable. She sighed for her lost ghost and began to eat her oatmeal, which by then was quite cold.

That night as she was settling down with *The Wizard of Oz,* Gamma materialized by her bed and said, "Child, I'm glad you have the habit of reading. It is mind-improving, but you don't have time for it now. We have much to attend to."

Emma Louise read on. She was not going to be fooled by a dream again. The book flew from her hands, and the next thing she knew it was lying on the bedside table closed.

"Mind your manners, child," the woman

scolded. "Speak when you are spoken to, and above all show some respect for your elders. After all," she added, and Emma Louise was sure she chuckled, "you can't get much elder than I."

"I didn't really mean to be rude," Emma Louise tried to explain. "But you're only a dream. I saw that this morning when I looked at my oatmeal."

"Tish, tosh, stuff and nonsense," the old woman exploded. "Must we go through that again? You are quite tiresome and perhaps not as bright as I thought. What does it take to convince you? Books don't fly through the air. How do you think that book got onto the table? Perhaps I will have to appear to someone else to get my task done."

"No, no, no," Emma Louise protested. "Don't do that. Please. I believe you, truly I do."

"Very well." Her great-great-grandmother was somewhat mollified. "But let's have no more nonsense. We have much to do." Her rocker suddenly appeared, and she sat down and started rocking at a furious pace.

"Well," she said at last, "as I said, we have much to do. I have been around town trying to get my bearings and formulate a plan, but it is discouraging. I can hardly make heads or tails of things. Most of the buildings are gone. Although the courthouse is still standing, they call it something else, and there is a monstrous ugly new courthouse for business purposes." Her eyes twinkled at Emma Louise as she said, "You and I might have a piece of business there, rather think that we will." She paused for a moment and then continued, "And this house, why it's right in town now. Time was when this house was way out with beautiful countryside all around, and all that countryside owned by my father Jeremiah Lewis. He owned a great part of the town too."

"You mean he was rich?" Emma Louise asked, surprised that one of her relatives could be anything but poor.

"He was certainly well to do," the woman answered somewhat proudly. "You needn't look so surprised. This house doesn't look like much now, and it wasn't a mansion even then. He didn't believe in putting on a show like some people I could mention, who go in debt to live high and mighty when in truth they don't have two dimes to rub against each other."

Emma Louise was interested in only one thing. "What happened to all the money?" she asked. "Why are we poor now? Was it inflation? Mom says inflation eats up money."

"That was not the case with this money," the little old woman snapped. "The truth is you were done out of it, my dear. Others are living in style on ill-gotten gains."

"Done out of it? You mean it was stolen?" Emma Louise asked incredulously.

"Well, yes," the woman replied. "In a manner of speaking that is just what I mean. It was stolen. You were robbed of your birthright by that conniving female Hettie Harris."

"Harris? You mean the Harrises of Harris Square?"

"I don't know anything about a Harris Square, but I would like to know who owns that big ugly mansion at the end of Cherry Street."

"Why, the Harrises, of course," Emma Louise answered. "They own just about everything in town. Harris Square, the big new shopping center. The bank, too. They are as rich as anything."

"That figures. It's as I suspected, only worse. We certainly have our work cut out for us. It will take some doing to right this wrong, but right it we will."

"Do what?" Emma Louise was puzzled. Sometimes Gamma was difficult to follow.

"Why, put you in the mansion at the end of Cherry Street and outfox Hettie Harris to boot."

"I can go in that mansion on Cherry Street any time I want." Emma Louise said. "Alice Harris is in my room at school. I don't like her much because she's prissy and stuck up, but she always invites me to her birthday parties, and I always go because she has the best birthday parties in town. She has movies, real live clowns, gallons of ice cream, oceans of coke, and mountains of cake

29

with surprises baked inside. Oh, I like her parties very much, although I don't like her very much at all."

"Well, I shouldn't wonder you don't like her. She's probably just like her great-great-grand-mother, Hettie Harris, and the saints them-selves couldn't have liked her. She was that conniving."

"Conniving?" Emma Louise repeated. She wasn't sure what that meant.

"Yes, indeed," the woman answered impa-tiently. "Cunning, deceitful, treacherous, call it anything you please. Always out to feather her nest, never mind the right or wrong of it. Oh, butter wouldn't melt in her mouth when she was talking to Adam, your great-great-grandfather. Always coming over trying to take charge during my last illness. Pretending to love my girls. I knew what she was up to. Knew she meant to marry Adam before I was cold in my grave. I tried to warn him. But men can be so simple about things like that, seeing only the smiling face of a two-faced woman." Once more the old woman seemed about to explode. She lapsed into silence, rocking furiously.

"Why on earth would she want to marry great-great-grandfather and take care of six children?" Emma Louise asked. "Didn't she have children of her own?"

Gamma fixed Emma Louise with a glittering eye. "The answer to your last question is the answer to your first question. Yes, indeedy, she had a child of her own, a worthless, spoiled son, name of Seth. He's why she wanted to marry Adam. Her own husband had died, scarcely leaving her a dime. She wanted my money for that no good son of hers. I knew Adam would be like a lamb led to the slaughter. So I made up my mind not to go on to the next world till I got things attended to in this one so my girls wouldn't be done out of their birthright. But first I had trouble appearing to people, and then I got locked in that trunk. Now you see I've got my work cut out for me." She shook her head sadly. "It's hard indeed to untangle nearly a hundred years of lies."

"Hettie Harris lied?" Emma Louise was trying hard to understand.

"I should say so. Hettie Harris, her son Seth, maybe Adam, too. But," she added somewhat grudgingly, "I don't know that I can blame Adam. I note from his tombstone that he died not long after I did. Rather sudden I believe, and rather suspiciously if you ask me."

"You mean Hettie Harris murdered great-great-grandfather?" Emma Louise asked in an awed tone.

The old woman did not answer at once but kept rocking back and forth. At last she said rather mysteriously, "We shall see what we shall see." After another moment of silence she went on, "But the important thing—my task—is to get my property away from those Harrises and back to the rightful owners." She fixed Emma Louise with her snapping eyes. "And that, of course, means you. It isn't fair for a great-great-grand-child and namesake of mine to be living as poor as a church mouse in a house going to rack and ruin while the descendants of that conniving Hettie Harris fatten on their ill-gotten gains."

"Alice Harris isn't fat," Emma Louise assured her. "In fact, she's kind of skinny."

"Must you be so literal?" Gamma asked. "Her size makes no never mind. Her bank account is fat enough. But we shall see what we shall see." She smiled a little secret sort of smile and said, "And he who laughs last laughs loudest."

"There is one thing I don't understand." Emma Louise said after a moment. "If the property was yours, how could Hettie Harris get it? What about your six girls?"

"Girls," the woman pounced on the word. "That's the whole point, they were girls. Girls carry no weight in court."

"Girls carry just as much weight as boys," Emma Louise protested. "Maybe they're not as heavy, but they certainly are just as important."

"You're absolutely right," the woman said. "Girls are just as important as boys. Always have been, always will be, but back when I was alive, it was men who ran things. They had women so tied up by laws and such that they could hardly do anything. Wouldn't even let them vote."

Gamma continued. "Hettie Harris was a widow with a son, Seth by name, a loud-mouthed irritating boy, if ever I saw one. Mean, too, used to swing cats around by their tails. He was a terrible boy, but clever in a wicked way. I'm sure the two of them, Hettie and Seth, figured out the scheme. Soon as I was out of the way, she managed by hook or by crook to marry my Adam. Then like as not Hettie and Seth forged Adam's name to a will leaving everything to Seth. And I'd be willing to wager they did a little something to hasten Adam's death."

"Wouldn't it have seemed strange to a judge," Emma Louise asked, "a father leaving everything to someone else's son and not leaving anything to his own daughters?"

"No," the woman shook her head. "The world has changed considerably. In my time it didn't seem strange at all. Seth was almost a grown man. Girls were judged to have no business sense whatsoever. Everyone would suppose he would look out for them."

"Then," Emma Louise said glumly, "that's that. I don't see that anything can be done about it now."

33

"Oh," chortled Gamma, "that's where you're wrong. That's where they all were wrong. The property was never Adam's to leave to anybody. It was mine, willed to me by my father. Under the law, my being a woman and married, my husband had the use of it in his lifetime, but it was never his to will to anyone. It was mine to will."

"To will?"

"Yes, to leave by law to whomever I chose, and that is exactly what I did. I made a will right there on my deathbed for I knew what Hettie had in mind. I got Joie, the cook, and Edna, the ironing woman, to be my witnesses. I made a will right and proper, as legal as you please. I left everything to my girls."

"But I don't understand," Emma Louise said. "If you made a will, and it was your property how could that other will give the property to Seth?"

The woman shook her head despairingly. "Use your head, child. No one saw my will."

"You mean no one knew about it?"

"Oh, they knew about it. I gave it to Adam. He could have the use of the property in his lifetime, then it all went to the girls, but my will was never acted on. Hettie saw to that. Got Adam in her clutches, poisoned him, destroyed my will, and put the fake will in its place. Oh, she was wicked."

"Then if she tore up your will," Emma Louise

34

sighed, her visions of riches vanishing, "there is nothing we can do. No one would ever believe this ghost story."

"Mind your tongue and don't sass me, young lady," Gamma said. Then, her eyes gleaming mischievously, she added, "The truth will out I've always said, and where there's a will there's a way." She laughed at her puns and leaned toward Emma Louise saying gleefully, "I outfoxed that Hettie Harris. I made two wills. I figured on such shenanigans as happened, happening. Now all we have to do is show the real will. And speaking of that, where is my desk? I've looked all over this house, and I can't find it."

"Desk?" Emma Louise asked. "We don't have any desk."

"Disposed of it, have you?" Gamma sounded somewhat discouraged. "That does make it more difficult." Then she brightened. "But I really shouldn't have expected to find it here. It was a fine piece of furniture. Like as not Hettie and her heirs made off with it. Probably sitting right now in that monstrous mansion on Cherry Street. Somehow or other you are going to have to get your hands on that desk. I hid the second will in it."

"In a secret drawer?" Emma Louise asked excitedly. She loved mystery stories with secret drawers.

"Of course not," Gamma answered scornfully. "Hettie would have been sure to find it there. I had Ebenezer the hired man hollow out one of the legs. He fixed it so no one would ever notice. Of course, I never let on to him my purpose, him having a wife Elvira who was the biggest gossip in six counties. I told him I was going to put my pearls in there for safekeeping. I knew when my pearls showed up on Hettie after my demise he would think no more about it."

"But if you kept it such a secret, what good was it? No one would know where to look for it."

"Oh, I told Faith in strictest confidence, her being my oldest child. She must have forgotten. She was a flighty forgetful sort of a girl. She and her chum Amity Edwards always were off in the clouds somewhere. By the way, I notice that the Edwards house is still standing. But to get back to what I was saying. Could be, Faith didn't believe me. Perhaps she thought my mind was fever wandering. I was very sick, you know."

Emma Louise didn't say anything. She was wondering where the desk was and how she could possibly get her hands on it.

She was startled when Gamma said, as if reading her thoughts, "Oh, you can find the desk. Go to the mansion on Cherry Street. You must also find a lawyer. He'll cost a pretty penny, always have, and I'm sure things haven't changed in that regard." She rocked vigorously for a moment and then said, "Enough of talk. Now is the time for action." She looked Emma Louise straight in the eyes. "What you must do is find the desk and get a lawyer. It's as simple as that."

"Wait, wait," Emma Louise said as Gamma seemed to be fading. "Don't go." But the tiny woman did not wait. As she disappeared, Emma Louise thought she heard her say faintly, "Use some gumption."

—IV—

Emma Louise thought it would take more than gumption. What if Hettie Harris did take the desk one hundred years ago? That didn't mean the Harrises still had it. And a lawyer? That was easier. Her mother had said that Robert E. Lee Grant III was a lawyer; his son Robert E. Lee Grant IV was in her class. The oldest boy of each generation of the Grant's was named Robert E. Lee, her mother had said, as a sort of a perpetual apology for having the name Grant, the Union general who defeated the South. Although the first sons were always named Robert E. Lee, they were never called that. Over the years R. E. Lee had become Relee. Now Robert E. Lee Grant III was called Big Relee, and Robert E. Lee Grant IV, Little Relee, everywhere but at school where Little Relee was simply Relee. Sometimes classmates would tease him by saying, "Oh, really, Relee?" But not often, for fighting was one of Relee's specialties. He'd had a lot of practice doing it.

After school the next day, Emma Louise looked for Relee to tell him about her family ghost and to ask his help. When she found him, he was about to have a fight with Timmy Henderson. From a safe distance Emma Louise shouted at him, "Relee, Miss Roth wants to see you."

Relee keeping his fists raised and his eyes squarely on Timmy said, "Yeah, who says so?"

"I say so," Emma Louise said as if she were telling the truth. After giving Timmy a mild shove, Relee walked back toward school with Emma Louise behind him. When they were a safe distance from the other boys, Emma Louise said, "Miss Roth doesn't really want to see you, Relee."

He turned and gave her a threatening look. "Now don't start that really-Relee business, and why did you say Miss Roth wanted me?"

Emma Louise didn't like the look in his eyes. She took a step back and said, "I didn't mean to start that really-Relee business. And I didn't mean to lie, but I have to talk to you. That's why I made up that story about Miss Roth."

His face relaxed a bit. "Yeah, what about?"

"About something important."

"I bet," Relee said and started walking away.

"Wait," Emma Louise cried, "I mean it, really I do, Relee."

He turned quickly and snapped, "I told you to cut that out."

"I'm sorry. I said that without thinking because I say 'really' a lot, but I do have to talk to you." Then she blurted out, "I need a lawyer."

"Yeah?" he said. "What did you do? Kill someone? Where did you hide the body?"

"Don't be like that," Emma Louise pleaded. "I do need a lawyer to help me get back some property my great-great-grandmother told me about." She was almost running to keep up.

"Where's the property?" he asked, more interested.

"Right here in town. Harris Square and some other places."

"Harris Square?" he laughed. "And how about Brooklyn Bridge? You're crazy."

"No, I'm not," Emma Louise insisted. "My great-great-grandmother told me so."

"You're even crazier than I thought. How could your great-great-grandmother tell you anything? She's dead, isn't she?"

"Well, yes," Emma Louise admitted somewhat reluctantly. "She's dead, but she's a ghost now. She comes to see me every night."

Relee stopped in his tracks and guffawed loudly. "Sure, I know. General Robert E. Lee comes to see me every night, my being his namesake and all." Then he said, "Now stop the kidding and bug off."

And Emma Louise did. She felt it was useless to say anything more.

That night when Gamma appeared Emma Louise was sitting up in bed waiting. "It's no use," she said despairingly. "I tried to get a lawyer, and I can't." Then she told about Relee and added, "Even if I could get a lawyer, I haven't the faintest idea how to look through the Harris house for the desk. Maybe I just don't have any gumption."

"Of course, you've got gumption, child," Gamma said. "But sometimes a little outside help is needed. For instance, we've got to make a believer out of that young friend of yours. What did you call him? Relee?"

"Yes, Relee, but he's no friend of mine. He doesn't even like me."

"If that's the case, he's not as bright as he should be, but we'll show him a thing or two. Doubts spirits does he? We shall see." She rocked briskly.

"Maybe if you appeared to him, Gamma, and explained everything?" Emma Louise suggested.

"No, I don't think a simple appearance would do for a boy like Relee. We'll have to frighten him a bit. Do him good, I expect."

"I can't frighten him," Emma Louise said. "He can lick any boy at school, even the bigger ones."

"I don't mean that kind of fright. No, I have something else in mind. Can you get him to the cemetery tomorrow night just after dark?"

"Maybe, I don't know for sure." Emma Louise said doubtfully.

"Certainly you can. Tell him you want him to meet your great-great-grandmother. Dare him to meet a ghost. If he's the boy I think he is, he won't pass up a dare."

When Emma Louise asked Relee to go to the graveyard he said, "Didn't I tell you to stop bugging me?"

"Yes, but my great-great-grandmother wants to meet you."

"I'll bet. General Robert E. Lee is also dying to meet you."

"Oh, all right," Emma Louise said, deciding to try the dare tactic. "I'll tell her you're scared to go to the graveyard after dark."

Relee grabbed her shoulder as she started to walk away and spun her around. "You think I'm scared to go? If anyone's scared it's you."

"I am not."

"You are too."

"OK, I'll show you. I'll be at the graveyard tonight," Emma Louise said, "but I bet you won't show up."

"I'll be there. I bet I don't see you."

Pleased, Emma Louise hurried away. She didn't want to smile in Relee's furious face.

——V——

That night as dark approached, Emma Louise was scared. At supper, she could not finish her carrots even though it meant she could not have chocolate pudding, her almost favorite dessert.

"Do you feel bad, dear?" Mrs. Jones asked.

Emma Louise shook her head.

"You look flushed. Perhaps you had better lie down for a bit. I'll do the dishes. Your homework can wait till later."

This suited Emma Louise fine. She went upstairs in case her mother might be watching. Instead of going to her room she slid down the bannister so she wouldn't make noises on the creaky old stairs and tiptoed to the front door.

On the dark tree-lined street that led to the graveyard, she felt her heart beating like a drum gone wild inside her chest. Once she stepped on a dry stick. The crackling sound it made frightened her so she almost fell down. Only the thought of what Relee would say the next day if she ran home made her keep walking.

During the day the cemetery held no fear for her. In the summer it was cool and pleasant. She had often visited Mr. Stewart the caretaker, who told her stories of times and people long ago. But night was different. As she approached the heavy iron gates which were locked at night, she walked more slowly. Were they to meet Gamma inside? What would she do?

Relee was nowhere in sight. Her spirits rose at the thought that he was too frightened to come and she could go home. Just as she was about to leave, he appeared.

"Over here," she whispered hoarsely from the shadows.

He jumped, then stood dead still peering into the darkness. Emma Louise moved toward him, almost forgetting her own fear, seeing Relee's reaction.

"Scared?" she teased.

"Course not," he answered. "I didn't see you. You surprised me."

"Sure, sure," she laughed.

"Come on, let's get this over with," he said and quickly scaled the wall and dropped down out of sight on the other side. Emma Louise tried to follow, but she couldn't get a toe hold in the crevices of the stones.

"What's the matter?" Relee asked in a loud whisper. "Scared?"

"No, I just keep slipping."

"Girls," he said disgustedly and climbed to the top of the wall to pull her up.

As soon as she was inside Emma Louise wished she were back outside. She was in a world of shadows. The tall trees were dark and still. Among them the tombstones gleamed whitely. In the eerie light of the rising moon, the stone angels guarding some of the graves cast almost human shadows.

"Well," Relee whispered hoarsely, "I'm here as I said I'd be, and your great-great-grandmother is not here as I said she wouldn't be. Now I'm going home."

"No," Emma Louise grabbed his hand. "We have to find her grave. Our family plot is over there under the tree with the branches that almost touch the ground. Come on."

Together they stepped into the moon-made shadows under the giant tree. Emma Louise stopped at a tombstone, leaned down and read the inscription.

"See, here it is," she said. "Emma Louise beloved wife and mother . . ."

The rest of her words were drowned out by an ear-piercing moan like something from a horror movie. Emma Louise forgot about being brave, about Relee, about her great-great-grandmother. She took off for the stone wall. She didn't see Relee pass her, but when she got to the wall he was on top waiting to give her a lift up.

In a somewhat shaky voice he said, "OK, you scared me. How did you do it? Did Mr. Stewart make the sound effects for you?"

Too out of breath to speak, Emma Louise shook her head and in a moment gasped, "Honest, Relee, I didn't do it. I was as scared as you. Maybe scareder."

"Then someone is playing tricks," Relee said, his voice quavering a little. Emma Louise didn't feel at all brave. Those sounds weren't what she expected from Gamma and if there were nice ghosts, then there could very well be scary ones too.

As Relee was helping Emma Louise scramble up the wall they heard someone cry as if in great pain and plead, "Please help me, please help me, get me out of here." The voice was faint but quite clear. They sat on the stone wall and looked at one another, poised to leap down to the other side.

"Maybe we should go for help," Emma Louise suggested.

Relee nodded, "But maybe we wouldn't have enough time. Maybe when we got back it would be too late." His voice trailed off in the faintest of whispers.

47

Emma Louise nodded. Again they heard the voice now sounding even weaker.

"We'll have to go ourselves," Relee said. He jumped down and crouched in the shadow of the wall. Emma Louise jumped and huddled beside him.

"Hunker down and keep in the shadows. Crawl on your stomach if you have to. We'll surprise them." Relee picked up two sticks and handed one to Emma Louise. "Here. Clobber them on the head from behind if you have to. The sounds are coming from near your family's graves."

Although they moved as quietly as possible, dry leaves cracking beneath their feet seemed to sound as loud as firecrackers. Suddenly a light shone around them. Emma Louise closed her eyes in terror. She could not bear to look at whatever kind of monster was bearing down on them. Then a familiar voice said, "Child, open your eyes. It's risky enough to blunder around in the dark without making matters worse by closing your eyes."

There, between two graves guarded by stone angels, sat Gamma calmly rocking in her chair. Relee, still in crawling position, stared at her, his mouth wide open, completely speechless. Emma Louise started shaking like a leaf. She was no longer scared, just weak and mad.

"It was you. All the time it was you," she said accusingly. "You made the monster sound and

then made us think someone was being killed. Do you think that's fun? I thought you were nice, but you're not."

"Who is she?" Relee asked, shaking his head from side to side. "I'm not believing this."

"She's my great-great-grandmother, that's who she is." Emma Louise was crying now. "Only she's not so great, and I don't care about righting old wrongs or getting back property. They can keep the whole town. I never want to see her again." She got up and started running toward the wall.

"Hold on a minute," Gamma commanded sternly. "That is no way to speak to your elders. But I'll forgive you, seeing there was some provocation. I had to test you to see if your friend here was equal to the job we have to do." She looked at Relee. "I had to make a believer of this young man since he didn't believe in spirits."

"That's right," said Relee, "and I'm still not sure I do. Anybody can play tricks."

"Oh, it's tricks you want is it?" said Gamma and disappeared. In a moment the stick Relee held was snatched from his hand. Then he was yanked around and the stick applied to his backside. He pulled away from the invisible grasp and started running, the stick chasing him all the way. Emma Louise stopped crying and began to laugh. Relee, running and stumbling in the moonlight, with nothing but a stick pursuing him was funny.

As suddenly as she had disappeared, Gamma reappeared. "Come back, young man," she said. And to Emma Louise, "Wipe those tears off your face. And you," she turned to Relee, "close your mouth. Don't stand there gaping. You look like a fish out of water." Relee sat on top of the wall, a dazed expression on his face. He reached down to help Emma Louise up. They looked down at the little woman once more rocking in her chair and looking up at them with a pleased expression on her face.

"You have both done well," she said. "Of course, you," she said to Emma Louise, "are a trifle too sassy, but we'll let that pass considering the circumstances. You were both brave, and I am proud of you."

Relee shook his head, "You're wrong. I wasn't brave. I was scared."

"Me, too," Emma Louise admitted.

"No, you're the ones who are wrong," Gamma replied. "Being brave has nothing to do with not being scared. Being brave is being scared but still doing what has to be done."

"Well, maybe so," Relee said, "but I've had enough of bravery and fright for one night. I'm going home."

"Not so fast, young man," Gamma commanded. "We have some things to attend to first." She looked at Emma Louise. "Mind your manners, child. Introduce me to your young friend."

"Gamma," Emma Louise began, "this is Robert E. Lee Grant the Fourth, but everybody calls him Relee."

Gamma peered at him. "Yes, yes," she said. "There is a family resemblance. Child, I knew your great-great-grandfather, Judge Grant, well. I wouldn't say you are the spitting image of him, but you do favor him a bit. Does the law still run in your family?"

Relee nodded.

"Good," Gamma was beaming, "for we shall have some legal matters to attend to before our business is finished. But first, you children must find my desk." Her voice seemed to trail away. "Oh, bother," she said, "scaring you young ones has worn me out. The tricking part of this spirit business takes an uncommon amount of energy. Tell this young man the details of our business," she commanded Emma Louise. "Now be off with you."

Gamma was gradually growing fainter. "Mind you hold your tongues about this for the present," she said before she disappeared completely. "No point blabbing to your parents till you have something to blab. Not that they'd believe you anyway." She chuckled and vanished.

As they walked home, Emma Louise told Relee everything she knew about her great-great-grandmother, her death, the desk, the will, and great-great-grandfather's marriage to Hettie Harris, his sudden and suspicious death, and about how Seth Harris had inherited all of her great-great-grandmother's property.

"When we find the will, we will need your father's help," she told Relee. But Relee was more interested in the long ago death of Emma Louise's great-great-grandfather.

"She thinks he was murdered, is that it?"

"Yes," Emma Louise said, "but that's not important now. Hettie Harris and her son died long ago. You can't arrest Alice Harris's father for what they did."

"No," Relee admitted, "but murder would show intent to defraud and make it easier to prove that the will giving the Harrises everything was a phony."

"You already sound like a lawyer," Emma Louise said. "Anyway that won't help unless we find the missing will."

"If we could prove he was murdered, people might listen to us," Relee said. "Maybe samples of his handwriting are in the records at the courthouse. Maybe we could get a handwriting expert to compare them with the phony will if that is still around."

"I don't know," Emma Louise shook her head doubtfully. "Those are a lot of 'maybes.' It's so long ago, we could never prove murder. The clues, even the people, are gone."

"Maybe so and maybe not," Relee said. "Maybe we could dig him up and find arsenic in his bones and hair."

"After all these years?"

"People's bones last a long time, and people used arsenic then, you know, like in that movie on TV last week. You know the one about the women who killed people and buried them in their cellar?"

"Yes, I know 'Arsenic and Old Lace,' but they were nice old women."

"Very nice. They had a cellar full of people they had been 'nice' to." They were silent for a moment, then Relee said, "She's right you know. We shouldn't tell anybody yet. They'd think we were crazy or making things up. In fact, tomorrow I might not believe it myself."

"I know," Emma Louise nodded. "When I first started seeing her I thought I was dreaming, but you saw tonight, she's as real as can be."

At the end of the dark street that led to the graveyard, they separated.

When Emma Louise got home, her mother was talking on the phone. The television was on too, so that Emma Louise was able to tiptoe upstairs without being heard.

54

No sooner was she in bed, than her mother came in to see how she felt. Looking at Emma Louise's cheeks rosy from the cold, she said, "You still look a bit flushed. You had best stay home from school tomorrow. There is a lot of flu going around."

——VI——

The next day Emma Louise caught up on her TV watching and didn't even think about ghosts and wills and desks, not even about Gamma, until 3:15 when Relee came peddling up to the house on his bicycle.

"Come on," he said, "let's go to Alice Harris's house and look for that desk."

"I can't," Emma Louise explained. "I stayed home sick today."

"You don't look sick to me," Relee said.

"I'm not really, Relee," Emma Louise admitted.

"Cut that really-Relee stuff," Relee said with a scowl.

"No, you cut it out." Emma Louise was irritated. "I can't be watching everything I say because of your old name. I use 'really' a lot just like I said."

"You sure do," Relee sounded grumpy. "Anyway, hurry up. Ask your mom if you can come out."

Although it took persuading, Emma Louise managed to convince her mother that fresh air and exercise were what she needed.

"How are we going to get into Alice's house?" she asked Relee as she bumped her bike down the porch steps. "Do we challenge her to a game of hide and seek? She'd never do it."

"I know," Relee admitted. "I don't think she ever does anything more exciting than play solitaire."

"She might not even be home. She might be having her piano lesson or her ballet lesson or a Girl Scout meeting. She's very programmed. If she is home, we'll have to be extra nice to her if we want to get inside the house."

"I suppose so, but it won't be easy," Relee grumbled. "I remember the time she told Miss Roth I put an ant down her back."

"Did you?"

"No, but I wish I had. Miss Roth made me stay after school and write 'I will not misbehave in class' five hundred times."

"She's a tattletale all right," Emma Louise nodded. "That's why we can't ask her whether she has an old desk. How are we going to look through the house?"

"Like on TV. One of us will distract her while the other looks."

Alice herself answered the doorbell and seemed surprised to see them.

"What do you two want?" she asked ungraciously. "You selling something like raffle tickets?"

"Why no," Emma Louise answered in her best lady-come-to-call manner. "We just thought we'd stop by to see you."

"What for?" Alice asked suspiciously.

"Why just to visit, of course." Emma Louise was still very ladylike. "May we come in?"

"Oh, all right," Alice said and led them down a richly carpeted hall to a large family room in which a TV was blaring.

"I was watching a great old monster movie."

"Wow," Relee said and sat down before the TV as if forgetting about old desks.

Emma Louise sat down, too. How were they to search the house? Was Alice's mother home?

"Doesn't having the TV on this loud bother your Mom?" she asked.

"No one's home but me. And I can watch anything as loud as I like as long as I like."

"That's great," Emma Louise said and meant it. In a moment she said, "Oh, look at my hands. I don't know what I could have done to get them so dirty. May I go wash up, Alice?"

"You know where," Alice answered not taking her eyes from the TV. Emma Louise walked quickly from room to room downstairs. There was no desk anywhere. She didn't have time to look upstairs.

When she got back Alice, having turned gracious hostess, looked at her kindly and said, "Oh, there you are. Relee and I were having a coke. Would you like one?"

"Yes, thank you," Emma Louise answered politely. While Alice was in the kitchen she whispered to Relee, "There's not a desk of any kind in the whole downstairs."

"Must be upstairs. Go look up there."

"I can't. I have no reason to go upstairs. Her mom might come home and catch me."

Alice was coming back, and Relee said quickly, "Wait till the monster movie is over, then I'll get up there."

When the movie ended, Relee turned to Alice and commented, "Boy, that was great." He looked around the room and said, "This room is something. I bet you do your homework here so you can watch TV while you work."

"Of course not, silly," Alice replied. "Mother would never let me. I do it up in my room."

"I bet you have it fixed up to study with a desk and everything," Relee said casually.

"Of course," Alice said proudly, "A desk, a desk light, all sorts of pens and pencils and paper, everything."

"I don't have a desk," Relee said. "I've been

thinking of asking for one for my birthday. But I'm not sure what kind."

"A desk is a desk," Alice said flatly. "It doesn't make much difference what kind you get."

"Oh, but it does make a difference," Emma Louise came to Relee's rescue. "There are rolltops, tabletops, drop-downs, and antiques, all kinds. I like the antique ones because I like old furniture. Is yours old?"

"It might be. I got it from Morrison's down at the Square."

"Then it's not an antique," Emma Louise said, a tinge of disappointment in her voice. "They only sell new stuff."

"Mother and Dad have antique desks," Alice said as Emma Louise and Relee appeared to lose interest.

"Where are they?" Relee asked.

"Upstairs, of course."

"I would just love to see them," Emma Louise gushed.

"I don't know," Alice was doubtful. "I'm not supposed to mess around in their things."

"Who's going to mess around?" said Relee. "Come on, Emma Louise, we've got to get going. I'll bet they aren't antique anyway. They're probably plain old desks."

Alice rose to he bait. "They are so antique," She insisted. "Wait," she cried as Relee and

Emma Louise headed for the door, "I'll show you they are antique. Come on upstairs."

"I don't know," Relee hesitated. "It's getting late."

Emma Louise nudged him. "We've got time if we hurry," she said and quickly followed Alice upstairs.

Alice displayed the desk in her father's study proudly. "See, I told you it was antique," she said.

Emma Louise didn't have the foggiest notion whether the desk was antique or not, but it was large and heavy and not what Gamma would have had. Relee examined it hurriedly and told Alice it was too large for his room.

The desk in the dressing room adjoining her mother's bedroom was very ladylike, delicate, and polished to a fine sheen. It just might be the one. Relee was equal to the occasion. Touching the desk admiringly, he said, "This is great. Only thing, it's kind of delicate. Maybe I'd be too rough." He fell on his knees and started thumping the legs.

"What are you doing?" Alice asked in alarm.

"Testing the strength of the legs," Relee explained. "They are as strong as can be." After a bit more thumping, he suddenly noticed the room had become strangely quiet. He pulled his head from under the desk and looked up to find Mrs. Harris staring down at him, an angry expression on her face.

"What do you think you are doing, young man?" she demanded. "And you, too, young lady?" she added including to Emma Louise in her wrath.

Timidly Alice tried to explain, "They were admiring your desk, Mama."

"Admiring my desk, indeed. I'll bet. Stand up, young man. Turn your pockets out."

"You don't think I was trying to take something from your old desk, do you?" Relee asked genuinely insulted.

"I know you young people. I know you are up to no good." Mrs. Harris leaned over and thrust her hands in first one pocket and then another. Then she gave him a small shake and quickly whisked her hands over Emma Louise.

"Come on, Emma Louise," Relee said, hardly able to contain his indignation, "Let's go. Why would we want anything from that old desk?"

"Not so fast, young man." Mrs. Harris seemed to fill the whole door. "You are Lawyer Grant's son, aren't you? He will hear about this. He should spend more time disciplining his own son instead of worrying about those ne'er-do-wells he defends in court. And you," she turned again to Emma Louise, "your mother is going to be disappointed in you, very disappointed indeed."

"We didn't do anything wrong so call them all you like," Relee almost shouted, his eyes blazing with anger. He grabbed Emma Louise's hand, squeezed past Mrs. Harris, and hurried from the house. Alice, trembly as a frightened bird, stood silently by her mother and watched them go.

As they bicycled away Emma Louise asked, "What do you think your dad will do to you?"

"Nothing, why should he? I didn't do anything," Relee's voice was extra loud, almost as if he were trying to convince himself.

"I don't know what Mom will do," Emma Louise said softly. "She'll be mortified I know. Mrs. Harris is always bragging about Alice, about her grades, her piano, her ballet. I guess I don't give Mom much reason to brag about me."

"Who wants to be bragged about?" Relee demanded scornfully. "And who would want to be a robot like Alice? She doesn't have a thought of her own except to tattle."

"I don't know. I felt sorry for her just now. I'm glad Mrs. Harris is not my mother."

"Me, too," Relee agreed. "With a mom like that you'd have your very own live-in monster."

At Emma Louise's turn off she asked, "What are you going to tell your dad we were doing with Mrs. Harris's desk?"

"I'll tell him I was checking it out 'cause I want one, just like I told Alice."

"Will he believe you—that you want a desk for your birthday?"

"I don't know. I'm in trouble either way. If he does believe me I'll probably get a desk for my birthday, and it's the last thing in the world I want. I'd rather have an HO racing set. If he doesn't believe me, I'm in for it."

"Then maybe what we should do is tell the truth about Gamma, the will, and the desk."

"Are you crazy? He'd never believe that."

"Well, then good luck."

"You, too."

But as he turned to leave, Emma Louise said, "Wait. We've got to decide where to look next, because I don't think it was Mrs. Harris's desk, do you?"

"No. None of the legs sounded hollow to me."

"Where can we possibly look?"

"I don't know. We'll have to figure something out."

"Oh, I know," Emma Louise said. "Miss Amanda's Antique Shop. She must have bunches and bunches of antique desks. We can still pretend you want one for your birthday."

"Sounds pretty good," Relee said after a moment's thought. "We'll check it out tomorrow, if we're not grounded because of Mrs. Harris."

——VII——

Miss Amanda's Antique Shop was in the front part of her well-kept old house. The broad porch, which Miss Amanda called the veranda, was used to display her antiques to passersby. As Emma Louise and Relee came up the steps, their eyes were caught by a huge rockinghorse, big enough for a nine-year-old to ride. Relee had thrown one leg over the horse when a voice said, "Careful, that horse hasn't been ridden for many a year. He might throw you." Startled, Relee jumped off, and he and Emma Louise looked around uncertainly to locate the voice.

"Don't just stand there gawking," the voice commanded. "Come in, come in." Timidly Emma Louise opened the door. The shadowy interior was crammed with a delightful assortment of strange things. By one of the windows that overlooked the porch sat Miss Amanda, a grand looking woman with snow white hair piled high on her head. Her blue eyes behind wire-rimmed glasses twinkled mischievously as she said to Relee, "Did I scare you?"

"Oh, no, not at all," he answered. "I wasn't going to ride the horse anyway. I'm too big for rockinghorses."

"Maybe so," she said, "but I feel that one could give you a good ride. He has been ridden to war and back many times in years gone by, I dare say."

Emma Louise and Relee fidgeted nervously from foot to foot.

Miss Amanda looked at them kindly. "Just what can I do for you? Can I show you something?"

Emma Louise's eyes riveted on a doll as large as a small child sitting in a fancy wicker carriage that had a pink silk umbrella on top.

"Oh," Miss Amanda said, following her gaze, "you like Victoria. She is a beauty, isn't she?"

Emma Louise nodded, then found her voice to say, "Her eyes look real, and she has real teeth not just ones painted on."

"Yes, she has for a fact," Miss Amanda agreed. "She is a French doll from the old days. Her eyes look real because they were made by the same people who made false eyes for people unfortunate enough to have lost their own." She picked up the doll and held it for Emma Louise to inspect.

"Does she break?" Relee asked looking at the delicate porcelain face.

"Very easily," Miss Amanda assured him.

"Then I don't know why anyone would want a doll like that. You'd have to be too careful for it to be fun."

"Oh, I'd want her," Emma Louise breathed, "to hold her and look at her. She's much too beautiful to throw around."

Relee turned from the doll to look into a room filled with old toys of all kinds. There was a train of the kind that ran when railroads were young, a circus with clowns and animals, a Noah's ark, a big handsome dollhouse, a cannon that looked as if it might really shoot, and a steam engine.

"Oh, boy," Relee said, "does that old steam engine really work?"

"I should imagine it does," Miss Amanda said leading the way into the room. "All these toys are in perfect condition."

"Where did you get them?" Relee asked.

"They came from Amity Edward's house. Poor soul died last summer. She was a hundred years old and lived all alone in that big old house by Harris Square. Did for herself too till the very end. She kept the nursery in that house just as it had been when she and her brother were children. He died young, you know. I hate to see that house go. I had hopes when she died that the town would buy it and turn it into a museum. That's out of the question though. Mr. Harris has the mortgage, and he plans to tear it down for additional parking space for Harris Square."

"Oh, no," Emma Louise cried. "That's almost my most favorite house in town. It looks like a fairy castle with that round tower."

"I call that a turret," said Miss Amanda. "It is a shame to see it go. It's a prime example of Victorian architecture."

"Can't anybody stop him?" Emma Louise asked.

"Stop Archibald Harris?" Miss Amanda gave a short mirthless laugh. "Small chance of that." Noting Emma Louise's face she added, "But things are never so bad that there is not a bright spot somewhere. These toys are worth a pretty penny, and Archibald Harris did not get them. The dear thing outwitted him on that. She gave them to me legal and proper years ago, but, of course, I never took them till she died. They stayed in the old nursery where they belonged. She wanted me to have them for she knew my dream of starting a museum for Lewisville. She gave me some other fine things, paintings and the like, to keep for the town to enjoy. My, how I ramble on. You children certainly aren't interested in such things. It's the horse that brought you to see me, isn't it? Browse through

68

the toys all you like, taking care of course."

"Ask her about the desk," Emma Louise nudged Relee.

Reluctantly Relee broke away from the toys and cleared his throat. "The toys are great, but what we really came in for is a desk. I'm looking for one for my birthday."

"Indeed," Miss Amanda said. "I shouldn't have imagined a boy like you would want a desk for his birthday. I would have thought something more like a racing set."

"No, it's a desk I really want," Relee insisted squirming a bit under her gaze.

"And you came here. How extraordinary. Why would you want an old desk?"

As Relee seemed unable to answer, Emma Louise said quickly, "He saw an old one that was really neat with secret drawers and everything."

"Oh, I see," Miss Amanda said and Emma Louise had the feeling she really did see much more than they intended. "I do have several very nice desks. I don't think I have any with secret drawers, or any really suitable for a boy, but come, I will show them to you."

Emma Louise and Relee followed her from room to room threading their way carefully through the maze of old things. Relee would look each desk over quickly, open and close the drawers, then drop down on his knees and thump the legs.

Miss Amanda watched him curiously, but said nothing until he had examined the last desk. Then in a kind but I-want-no-nonsense way she demanded, "Just what are you looking for? It certainly is not secret drawers, and I don't even think it is a desk." Relee turned bright red and looked helplessly at Emma Louise.

Emma Louise didn't want to lie to Miss Amanda. She liked her. Feeling she was someone they could trust she blurted out, "Yes, we are looking for something. We're looking for a will hidden in the leg of a desk."

"Come on," Relee urged Emma Louise, "she won't believe us. She'll think we're crazy."

"Maybe I will and maybe I won't, but you won't know till you've tried me. Let's sit down, and you can tell me the whole story."

In great rushes of words they told her about Gamma, the Harrises, and the will. When they had finished they watched her face anxiously, but she only looked thoughtful.

"You do believe us, don't you?" Emma Louise asked unable to take the silence.

Miss Amanda began to speak slowly, choosing her words carefully, "Yes, I do believe you. I can't say that I believe in ghosts in the usual sense of the word, but I do think that there are more things in life than most of us have dreamed of, and I do believe in extrasensory perception. Some individuals have the ability to sense and feel things most people cannot perceive. You children have that ability. I believe some important information has been communicated to you. Exactly how I don't know, but I believe there is truth in what you have perceived. Somewhere, I'm sure there is a desk with a hollow leg that has a will inside. I aim to help you find it."

Emma Louise felt like jumping up and hugging Miss Amanda. Now that an adult knew and believed their secret, she felt as if a great weight had been lifted from her shoulders.

"Do you really think we can find it?" Relee asked.

"If it hasn't been destroyed, and if it's still round Lewisville. I could have saved you a lot of time and thumping by telling you none of the desks I have is what you're looking for. I know the history of each of them. But it's getting late, and you children don't want to worry your folks. You had better run along."

——VIII——

Emma Louise was excited and happy waiting for Gamma that night. She thought she would be pleased that Miss Amanda was going to help them find the desk.

"Hummp," Gamma said, not overjoyed at all. "I guess you had no choice but to tell that woman, considering the circumstances. I hope she is a body that can hold her tongue. No point in getting other tongues wagging."

"We can trust her," Emma Louise said, "I know we can. She believes I have extrasensory perception."

"So that's what she believes, is it?" Gamma wasn't impressed. "Couldn't believe in anything as ordinary as spirits, I suppose."

"I think that is what she really believes," Emma Louise said. "She just puts it a different way."

"Maybe so, maybe so. Perhaps she will be useful to us. Now you and the boy can concentrate on other things."

"Oh, I know she will be useful to us. She knows about old things. You ought to see her shop. She has old toys and things that belonged to old Miss Edwards."

"Edwards?" Gamma repeated. "I wonder if that could be Amity Edwards who was Faith's best friend."

"I don't know," Emma Louise answered. Then she added, "She lived in the fairy-tale house by Harris Square, only, Harris Square must not have been there then."

"Certainly not," Gamma sniffed. "The Harrises did not have their ill-gotten gains then. You no doubt mean the house with the turret. That was the home of Amity Edwards, Faith's friend. My, it's hard to think that little Amity has grown old and gray."

"And dead," Emma Louise put in.

"You hadn't mentioned that, but it's not surprising. She would be quite old by my calculations, but enough of that. You and I have things to do. In the attic we must find a sample of handwriting. Letters, I suppose, will do. Then you and your friend can go to the courthouse and find the will that gave everything to Seth Harris. We will do a little comparing. I'm sure forgery will out."

Even though Emma Louise wasn't anxious to go to the dark attic she followed Gamma, shivering a little as her feet touched the icy floor.

The next day she could hardly wait for school to be out to tell Relee about the old letters in her great-great-grandfather's handwriting, but Relee had news of his own.

"Guess who's back in town?" Before Emma Louise could answer, he said, "Alice Harris's brother Seth."

"Sonny Harris?"

"Yeah, only they don't call him Sonny anymore; they call him Seth."

Emma Louise's mouth dropped open. "I didn't know his real name was Seth. That's really a coincidence. Seth was the name of the no good boy who got all our money."

"This is another no good Seth Harris," Relee chortled. "He's meaner than anything. He and three or four other guys rode into town on their motorcycles practically running everyone down. Mrs. Harris won't let them in the house. Only Marilyn Monroe Hicks will have anything to do with them. Bud Winters says she used to go with Seth before he dropped out of school. He says the Harrises told Seth then that he had to go to school or get out of town, so he left. But he's back now and meaner than ever."

A nervous shiver tingled over Emma Louise,

and she said, "I wonder what he will do to us if he finds out what we are doing?"

"Don't worry about that," Relee said. "He'll never know anything until everything is finished. Then there won't be any point in his doing anything to us."

"There's still lots to do before it's over and done," Emma Louise said, still feeling odd deep inside. "Are you grounded because of Mrs. Harris?"

"Dad didn't even say anything about it," Relee said, shaking his head. "Are you?"

"Mom didn't say anything either." Emma Louise was puzzled. "I can't understand it. Mrs. Harris was so mad. I thought sure we were in for terrible trouble."

"Me, too," Relee admitted. "Maybe when old Seth blew back into town she got so discombobulated she forgot."

"That must be it," Emma Louise agreed, "but she might remember it at any time. We had better work fast while we can. And I have something we can work with. We may not have to find the desk and will. Look at these," she said, taking some letters from her notebook. "They're letters in my great-great-grandfather's handwriting. There is his signature. If we can compare this writing with that on the will and prove that it was a forgery, maybe people will believe us."

Relee took the old papers and sat down on a bench by the bikerack. "Boy, these are old," he said.

"I know. They were in the trunk in the attic. We can take them down to the courthouse. That's where the will would be, isn't it?"

"Of course, they keep old records from way back. This will be easy as anything."

"Maybe not," Emma Louise said. "They don't let just anybody in to poke around, do they?"

"No problem," Relee waved her doubts aside, "I know the record clerk. "We'll tell him we have to do research for a history composition. People are always researching in those old records. Come on," he said, hopping on his bicycle. "Let's go now."

——IX——

Relee was right. John Smith, the record clerk, was so helpful that it made Emma Louise feel guilty to fool him. When Relee explained they were interested in the records from 1850 to 1900, he took them back to a musty room and showed them how the records were stored.

"Hot dog," Relee exulted when he left. "We'll have this over in no time."

But it wasn't easy. It was frustrating.

"Oh, darn," Relee said, "I wish I had asked him right out to show us the wills from the year your great-great-grandfather died. When did he die?"

"I'm not sure," Emma Louise admitted.

"For Pete's sake. You should know something as important as that."

"I don't think it's so important," Emma Louise defended herself. "Names are what's important. Aren't files arranged by name? I know his name was Adam J. Atkins, and the will left everything to Seth Harris. Oh, this is hopeless. Maybe we're going to have to depend on Miss Amanda's finding the desk."

Just then they heard a muffled sneeze.

"Somebody's in here with us," Relee whispered.

"Let's go," Emma Louise urged. She felt like a burglar caught in the act.

"What's to be afraid of?" Relee whispered. "Mr. Smith brought us, didn't he? We have every right to be here, and I'm staying till we find what we came to find."

"But who do you think it is?" Emma Louise felt as if her heart were pounding loud enough to drown out the whisper of her words.

"Probably someone else doing research," Relee said. "They do it all the time. I wish I could find the wills." He continued moving from one file to another.

Emma Louise could only think of that muffled sneeze. Someone had heard every word. What had been said? Had they given their secret away?

Relee was wandering around aimlessly and getting more frustrated by the minute. Emma Louise followed closely. Rounding a filing cabinet in a particularly dim corner of the room, they almost fell over a girl sitting on a low stool. There had been no evidence of her presence. No pages turning, no cabinets being opened.

She stood up and looking very tall, glared down at them. "Why don't you kids look where you are going?" she demanded.

"I'm sorry," Emma Louise stammered. "It's dark in here, and we didn't see you."

"Thought you had the place all to yourselves, didn't you?" the girl responded.

"We said we were sorry," Relee grabbed Emma Louise's arm and started to walk away.

"Not so fast," the girl said, "just what have you kids been doing? You aren't supposed to be here. I've a good mind to call the sheriff."

Despite Emma Louise's pulling at Relee's arm, he turned to face the girl. "Go ahead and call him," he said. "Mr. Smith brought us down here. We're doing research for school."

The girl had followed them from the dim corner. In the brighter light Emma Louise saw that she had masses of yellow hair, red lips, and eyelashes thick with mascara. She loomed over them threateningly.

"Research," she laughed derisively. "Ha. What do you know about research? I don't recall when I was in school that there was a class on wills. Or maybe," she taunted Relee, "maybe you're already practicing law with your paw. I wonder how much Mr. Smith knows about this will business."

Emma Louise was edging toward the door, and Relee began to follow her.

Once they were in the hall outside Emma Louise whispered, "Do you think she knows?"

"I don't know," Relee answered. "I don't remember what we said. I hope we didn't say too much. We'd be in trouble for sure."

"Do you think she will go to the sheriff?"

"Not likely. Don't you know who she is?"

Emma Louise shook her head.

"That's Marilyn Monroe Hicks. She's some kind of file clerk here. She was Seth Harris's girl before he left town."

When they got outside a lot of the worry left Emma Louise. "Oh, well, I guess it really doesn't make any difference to her what we were looking for," she shrugged her shoulders. "She was just being mean trying to scare us like that."

"Maybe she wasn't just being mean," Relee mused. "Maybe she really doesn't want us to come back. We said something about the will and the Harrises, I think."

"But even if we did," Emma Louise was beginning to feel better the farther they got from the courthouse. "What difference could it make to her?"

"Don't you remember I told you she used to be Seth Harris's girl friend? Probably still is."

"But we didn't say anything about trying to prove the will a forgery. Anyway she doesn't know the Harris property came from my great-great-grandfather."

"I suppose not," Relee agreed. "But she is a nosy, poky person who tells everything she knows. I hope she doesn't realize she knows something special, because she wouldn't keep her mouth shut, and we'd be in for trouble."

That night as Emma Louise was getting ready for bed she almost hoped Gamma would not appear. She didn't want to tell her they hadn't found anything at the courthouse. However when she came back into her room after brushing her teeth, Gamma was rocking happily in her chair, an inquisitive look on her face. Emma Louise gave her a brief smile of welcome and crawled into bed.

"Come, come, child," the old woman said impatiently, "speak up. Tell me about the will. It was a forgery, wasn't it?"

"I don't know," Emma Louise answered, her voice hardly more than a whisper.

"For pity's sake, child, you will have to speak louder than that. Only a mouse could hear you."

"I don't know," Emma Louise repeated loudly holding her breath. But Gamma didn't seem particularly upset.

"You mean you haven't had a chance to have an expert compare the writing?" she prodded.

"No." Emma Louise took a deep breath then rushed on, "I mean we couldn't find the will. Oh, we got into the record place, but it was so confusing. There must be a hundred million trillion records. We didn't know where to look. We didn't even know when great-great-grandfather died. And when we were trying to find something we stumbled on Marilyn Monroe Hicks, who told us we had better get out or she would make trouble."

Gamma's eyes were snapping, but when she spoke her voice was kind. Her wrath was directed at someone else.

"This Marilyn Monroe Hicks," she asked, "who is she, and what authority does she have at the courthouse? Seems to me there were no Hicks here in my time."

"I think her family moved here when she was little. Relee says she is a file clerk down at the courthouse. He says she used to be Seth Harris's girl."

"Seth Harris!" Gamma exclaimed. The name had startled her so she almost jumped out of her chair.

"Oh, not your Seth Harris, who poisoned great-great-grandfather," Emma Louise laughed. "This one is alive. He left town, but now he's back. Relee says he brought some other guys with him, and they all have motorcycles."

"Motorcycles?" Gamma repeated questioningly.

"Yes," said Emma Louise, "you know, motorcycles."

"No, I don't, although I have seen strange things in this town like horseless carriages going up and down the streets. Is that what you mean?"

"Oh, no, those are cars." Emma Louise was surprised at Gamma's ignorance of such matters. "A motorcycle is like a bicycle with a motor. The motor makes things go," she explained kindly.

"An invention of the devil, no doubt. But enough of that." Gamma waved her hand dismissing the subject. "I am concerned about this present-day Seth Harris. If he is at all like his ancestor, he will be up to no good. He will bear close watching. You say his girl friend was eavesdropping while you and Relee searched the records? What did she hear?"

"I don't know," Emma Louise admitted. "I can't remember what we said. Relee thinks we mentioned great-great-grandfather's will and the Harrises, but that shouldn't mean anything to her."

"Maybe so and maybe not," Gamma said. "We had best attend to our business quickly. Tomorrow you go back to Miss Amanda to see if she has made any progress. Perhaps we can work from that angle." She was rocking swiftly but getting dimmer and dimmer. In a moment Emma Louise was alone in her room.

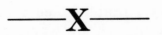

X

The next day Miss Amanda had nothing encouraging to report. She followed Emma Louise and Relee onto the broad front porch. "You mustn't lose heart because we haven't found the desk," she said. "It takes time to locate things that have been missing close to a hundred years. But never you worry, if it's around we'll find it. I'm certain of that." They left very encouraged and in just moments a figure crawled from beneath Miss Amanda's porch and stole stealthily away.

Because Emma Louise and Relee had such confidence in Miss Amanda, they were not surprised when they found a note from her the next day after school. It was in a white envelope taped to the seat of Relee's bike. Typewritten, it was brief, "I think I have located the desk. It's in the old Harvey house on Lonesome Bluff. Meet me there after school."

"Hot dog," Relee whooped. "Now we're getting somewhere. Let's go."

"We can't go right now," Emma Louise objected. "I didn't ride my bike, and it's too far to walk. I'll have to go home first."

"We can't do that," Relee protested. "Your mom would want to know where we were going. We don't have time to waste. Lonesome Bluff is a long way, and it gets dark early now."

"It is a long way," Emma Louise said thoughtfully. "Why didn't Miss Amanda stop by and take us?"

"She probably had to go out that way on business first and couldn't wait," Relee reasoned. "You know how she hauls stuff all over the country in that truck of hers. We'll ride double out there, and I can put my bike in the back of the truck and ride home with her."

It was getting rather late when they got to the old Harvey house. Shadows were beginning to fill the potholes in the road. Emma Louise was riding on the handlebars and she was joggled and thumped with every bump, and Relee's legs ached. But when they arrived at the deserted house, Miss Amanda's truck was nowhere in sight.

"Oh, no," Relee groaned, "it took us so long, she gave up and went back to town."

"We didn't meet her on the road," Emma

Louise pointed out. "We only passed the mail-man."

"Maybe she didn't go back to town. Maybe she went over to Crosston."

"I suppose so."

"Or," Relee brightened, "maybe she is here. Maybe some one dropped her off and is coming back for her."

"Who would be coming way out here?"

"The people who told her about the desk."

"They wouldn't leave her here."

"If they had to go somewhere while she was waiting for us they would. There's one way to find out. We can go look."

"No," Emma Louise said flatly. The sun had almost set, and the house, shaded by old cedar trees, was ominously dark. "There's no point in going in. She's not here. She would have been watching for us and heard us talking and come out."

"I guess you're right," Relee said. "We might as well go home."

"Do you want to rest a minute before we start?" Emma Louise asked.

"I'm not tired," Relee answered.

They started down the twisting lane that led from the house to the road. As they rounded the last turn, they found the way blocked by three motorcycles placed end to end, but no one was in sight. Tall weeds lined either side of the lane so there was no way to ride around the motorcycles. Emma Louise's heart began to pound frantically.

"Quick," Relee whispered, "let's carry the bike around." As they were doing this, a deep voice called from the dark shadows of the nearby woods, "You kids didn't stay long. Couldn't you find what you were looking for?"

"Hurry," Relee urged. Emma Louise tried, but the weeds were thick and kept catching in the spokes of the bike wheels. Frantically they tugged.

"Oh, come now, what's your hurry?" the voice continued. "Seems a shame to come way out here for such a short visit."

They were almost around the motorcycles, when the owner of the voice came out of the woods. It was Seth Harris, and he was as big as his voice. And the two fellows with him were equally as large.

"Don't bother putting that bike on the road, kids," Seth Harris said. "You're not going anywhere." He grabbed the bike, threw it on the ground, and the three kicked it with their heavy boots. In moments the bike was in no condition to ride.

"What a shame," Seth taunted, "your bike had a little accident. How lucky you two weren't on it. Wouldn't it be a shame if these two kids had a little accident?"

"Yes," his friends agreed, "a real shame."

"But I'm sure they wouldn't want that," Seth continued. "I'm sure they're going to come with us and tell us why they want to poke around at the courthouse and hunt for desks with their antique lady friend."

He grabbed Relee who began yelling, "Let go of me, let go of me."

"Cut that out," Seth said roughly, giving Relee a sharp slap across the face. He reached into the pocket of his jeans, took out a rag that looked as if it had been used to polish his motorcycle, and stuffed it into Relee's mouth.

"Let go of him," Emma Louise yelled and kicked Seth in the shin.

"You little devil," Seth snarled and cuffed her soundly on the cheek. "Grab her and stuff something in her mouth," he directed his friends. "We'll take them to the bluff. I don't want anybody to hear them yell." He swung Relee across his shoulders holding him securely by the legs. "Mike, you take the girl," he directed the taller of his friends.

Hanging loosely, Emma Louise tried to hit Mike across the back, but many of her blows missed. Relee was able to pummel Seth so much that Seth stopped and told his other friend to go back to the motorcycles for rope. He tied the legs and hands of both Relee and Emma Louise, and the trio proceeded on through the woods carrying their captives. By now it was getting very dark.

In a clearing overlooking the river, Seth dropped Relee to the ground and motioned for Mike to do the same with Emma Louise. "Now, we'll get to the bottom of this will and desk business," he said. He turned Relee over roughly with his foot, reached down, and pulled the rag from his mouth.

"Let me go, let go," Relee demanded immediately.

"Yell all you want, kid," Seth laughed. "Nobody is going to hear you out here. We'll wait till you get it out of your system. We've got all the time in the world, and you aren't going anywhere."

"I'm not going to tell you anything," Relee answered.

"Going to be a hero in front of your girl friend, is that it? I'll tell you what we'll do about that. We'll just get rid of your girl friend so you don't have to be a hero. Mike, throw her over the cliff," Seth said abruptly.

"You're bluffing," Relee said. "You don't dare throw her over. They'd get you for murder."

"What do you think about that, Mike?" Seth asked. "Think the police would take us in for murder?"

"They'd have to catch us first," Mike laughed.

"Oh, no," Seth said. "They wouldn't have to catch us. We wouldn't go anywhere except back to town to tell how we saw these two kids scuffling and how they accidentally fell over the bluff. Good citizens reporting an accident. The sheriff would be pleased. Now, kid, spit it out. What's this will and desk business?"

"I'm not going to tell you." Although his words were positive, Relee's voice quavered.

Seth turned to Mike. "I thought I told you to throw that kid over the bluff."

"Sure, sure," Mike answered and grabbed Emma Louise. "I thought you weren't ready, Seth."

"I am now," Seth responded. "We have to show this little hero we mean business."

Twisting and squirming, Emma Louise tried to get away from Mike and to get the oily rag out of her mouth.

"Just a minute, Seth," Ed said, "I think the girl's trying to tell us something. Maybe she doesn't want to go over the bluff. Maybe she's smarter than dum-dum here."

"Good thinking, Ed," Seth said. He leaned over and pulled the rag from Emma Louise's mouth. She began spitting to get rid of the dirty oily taste.

"Here, here," Seth protested. "Look at her spitting. I thought she was a lady."

"You'd spit, too, if you had that dirty thing stuffed in your mouth," Emma Louise said. "Now untie me and let me go."

"Well, now just where have I heard that

before? Sister, you're not going anywhere except over that bluff like I said. Unless, of course, you want to be smart and tell us what we're interested in."

"I won't tell you anything." Emma Louise was so mad and scared she forgot to be cautious. "Gamma was right. My great-great-grandfather was murdered by your great-grandfather."

"Emma Louise," Relee implored, "stop. Don't say any more."

"Shut up," Seth said and gave Relee a hard kick on the thigh. He turned to Emma Louise. "What's this about murder?" When Emma Louise didn't answer, Seth grabbed her hair and began dragging her to the edge of the bluff. "Maybe the view from here will loosen your tongue."

"Seth, she's just a dumb little kid," Ed said. "She doesn't know anything. I bet that girl friend of yours was spacing-out telling you about an old will, and what if these kids are trying to locate some old desk? That doesn't mean anything."

"Who gives the orders around here?" Seth snarled.

"You, of course, Seth," Ed said. "But that doesn't include murder."

"I always suspected you were a little chicken," Seth taunted. Once more he started pushing Emma Louise toward the edge of the bluff, rolling her over and over with his foot to the accompaniment of Relee's screams.

Suddenly Seth stopped, whirled around, and glared at his friends. "Getting coy and smart aren't you? OK, which one of you did it?"

"Did what?" they both demanded.

"Pinched me."

"Not me," said Mike.

"Me neither," Ed answered.

Seth turned back to Emma Louise, but before he could push her farther, he screamed and whirled on the other two. "OK, that does it," he said advancing toward them. "Now you're not going to say one of you didn't hit me with a stick?"

"I didn't," Ed protested.

"Me neither," said Mike.

"In it together? Think the two of you can take me on?" As Emma Louise, Relee, and the other two watched, a stick, seeming to come from nowhere, struck Seth squarely on the jaw, swung back, then struck him again and again.

Seth, lunging away from the stick, shoved his fist at Ed's face.

"I'm not hitting you, Seth," Ed protested. "See, I don't have any stick in my hand. It's dark but not that dark. That stick is hitting you by itself. I've never seen anything like it." He turned and started running through the woods toward the road with Mike behind him.

The stick continued to beat Seth soundly, front and rear. Seeing no assailant, Seth began to whimper, "Help me. Somebody help me," his voice becoming more desperate. He, too, began running toward the road, the stick still pursuing him.

Emma Louise turned toward Relee, barely visible in the dark. "Good old Gamma," she said. "She came to the rescue."

"I hope she quits chasing them long enough to come and untie us," Relee said.

But moments passed before Emma Louise and Relee saw lights flickering through the woods toward them.

"Do you suppose they're coming back to finish us off ?" Relee asked.

Then from the woods a voice said, "They must be in the clearing." Emma Louise went limp with relief for the voice was not that of Seth or his friends.

"Over here, over here," Relee called. Emma Louise, crying softly, could not say a word.

──XI──

Sheriff Bailey was gruff but kind. After making arrangements for Seth and his companions to be taken into custody, he drove the children back to town.

"Your folks are waiting at the courthouse," he said. "Disappearing as you did stirred things up. Lucky for you the postman saw you headed toward Lonesome Bluff. Your parents didn't know where to look for you. You've been through a bad time, but I've got a few questions that need answers. Let's start with why you went to a place like Lonesome Bluff by yourselves so late in the day without telling your folks or anybody else?"

"We were going to meet Miss Amanda," Emma Louise answered.

"Miss Amanda?" the sheriff sounded surprised. "What has she got to do with this?"

"She left us a note on my bicycle to meet her at

the old Harvey house," Relee explained. By now they had reached the courthouse where Mrs. Jones and Mr. and Mrs. Grant were waiting.

After tearful hugs and kisses, Mrs. Jones dried her eyes and in a puzzled voice echoed Sheriff Bailey's question, "Emma Louise, why in the world did you go out there without a word to me?"

Mrs. Grant, looking at Relee, said, "That is exactly what I want to know."

"That's what I have been trying to find out," the sheriff said. "Perhaps we had all better go into my office and get to the bottom of this." He turned to a deputy. "Go ask Miss Amanda to step over to my office for a bit."

Sheriff Bailey led Emma Louise, Relee, and the parents into the courthouse. When all were in his office, he explained, "The children say they got a note from Miss Amanda asking them to meet her out there."

"That's right, we did," put in Relee.

"Whatever for?" Mrs. Jones questioned.

"How very odd," said Mrs. Grant.

"Note or no note," Mr. Grant said, "there is no excuse for going off without informing your mothers."

"But we didn't have time. It was going to get dark," Relee tried to explain.

"What was out there that couldn't wait?" Mr. Grant asked sternly.

"We thought Miss Amanda was, and we

97

expected her to bring us back on her truck with the desk."

"What desk?" Mrs. Jones was more puzzled than ever.

"Yes, what desk?" the others wanted to know.

Before Emma Louise and Relee could answer, Miss Amanda walked through the door. "Are the children all right?" she asked anxiously.

"Right as rain," the sheriff assured her. "Seth Harris and his friends roughed them up a bit, but no real harm was done. I sent for you, Miss Amanda, to help us get to the bottom of this matter. The children say you left them a note to meet you at the old Harvey place."

Miss Amanda turned to the children, a look of bewilderment on her face. "I sent you no note," she said.

"Remember," Relee prompted, "the note about finding the desk?"

"But I haven't found the desk, and I sent no note," Miss Amanda said positively.

"I don't understand," Emma Louise was puzzled. "The note said to meet you there."

"Now, children," the sheriff put in, "Honesty is always best. You made a mistake going out there, but you are making things worse by trying to blame Miss Amanda."

"We're not trying to blame Miss Amanda," Relee insisted. "If she says she didn't leave the note, then she didn't leave it, but someone did, because we got a note. Wait a minute. I can prove it. It's in my notebook."

"But, Relee," Emma Louise reminded him, "your notebook fell out of your basket when Seth Harris stomped on your bike."

"Yeah, I guess it's lost in the weeds out there."

"Don't worry, son," Mr. Grant said and gave Relee a reassuring pat on the shoulder. "I believe you and I'll go now and find that notebook."

"No need for that," the sheriff said. "I had someone bring in the bike. They probably got the notebook, too." He spoke briefly into the phone on his desk.

In moments a deputy came in with Relee's notebook. It was dirty and battered, but when Relee looked inside the note was still there.

"That's a typewritten note," Miss Amanda said. "My name is just typed at the end. Don't you two know I would never ask you to go to a lonely place like the Harvey house by yourselves? But who did send that note? Who besides the three of us knew about that desk?"

Emma Louise said thoughtfully, "Marilyn Monroe Hicks knew about the will. Do you suppose she knew about the desk, too?"

"Desk? Will?" Mrs. Jones asked. "Will somebody please tell me what's going on?"

"That is something we all want to know." Mr. Grant looked at Relee. "Suppose you begin at the beginning, son, and tell us what this is all about."

Relee looked at Emma Louise questioningly. "We might as well tell them," she said. "Everything is such a mess we have to. Gamma will understand."

"Gamma?" Mrs. Jones asked.

"Yes. She has never appeared to you, Mom. She is my great-great-grandmother, and she told me about a family desk that has a missing will. It would prove great-great-grandfather's will which left everything to the Harrises was a forgery. Gamma says we are the rightful heirs."

Mrs. Jones and the others sat in stunned silence. Before they could speak, Relee, who had been puzzling over the note said, "Seth Harris must have sent the note. He had to, for how else would he have known we were there? We only passed the postman on the road."

"Maybe I can answer that," the sheriff said. "Seth Harris and those two friends of his have been living in that old house since he came back to town."

"I still think he sent it," Relee insisted.

"Me, too," Emma Louise agreed. "Marilyn Monroe Hicks must have told him we thought my great-great-grandfather's will was a forgery."

"Forged wills, missing desks," Mr. Grant said

100

incredulously. "You two have been watching too much television."

"But you don't understand," Emma Louise's voice was desperate. "It's all true. The will was forged by Seth Harris and his mother. Not this Seth Harris, his great-grandfather. The real will is hidden in my great-great-grandmother's desk. That's why we've got to find it."

Everyone was looking at Emma Louise and Relee as if they had taken leave of their senses.

"Emma Louise," her mother said, shaking her head in disbelief, "you have always been a normal, reasonable child. Why have you come up with this ghost story?"

"Maybe I don't exactly believe in ghosts," Miss Amanda spoke up in their defense, "but I believe what the children are saying. I think we can find that will and that it will verify what they say. In the meantime, sheriff, I think you should make that note secure.

"Ghost stories aside," Mr. Grant looked at the sheriff, "it does appear someone tried to lure the children out to that old house. Perhaps it was just a prank, but it warrants investigating."

"Prank?" Relee's voice cracked with indignation. "Some prank. Why they were going to throw Emma Louise over the bluff."

"Son," Mr. Grant said, "I think you are overwrought."

"I'm not, I'm telling the truth."

Mr. Grant motioned him to be silent and continued addressing the sheriff. "Presumably the note was written to lure the children to Lonesome Bluff."

"It just doesn't make sense," Mrs. Jones shook her head. "Why would anyone go to all that trouble to get the children out to Lonesome Bluff?"

"But I told you, Mom," Emma Louise said, "they don't want us to find out about the will. That's why they tried to kill us."

"Hold on there, young lady," the sheriff admonished, "that's a serious charge you're making. I know those young hoodlums roughed you up a bit, but it's hard to believe they meant murder. The boy is a Harris, and things like that don't happen here."

"But it did," Relee insisted. "They were going to throw Emma Louise over the bluff if I didn't tell them what we know."

"They didn't, did they?" The sheriff spoke as one reasoning with a willful child. "When we got there they were headed to the house, and rather fast as I remember."

"That's because Gamma chased them off."

"Gamma?" Mr. Grant questioned.

"I think they mean this friendly family ghost they've been telling us about," the sheriff said almost teasingly.

The grownups looked at one another, smiling and shaking their heads.

"Dear, I do believe you are so overwrought you don't know what you're saying," Emma Louise's mother said, putting a comforting arm around her.

"You're absolutely right, Mrs. Jones," Relee's father agreed. "They've been through enough to make them distraught. Let's have no more questioning while they are in this state. The best thing is get them home to bed."

All the grownups except Miss Amanda agreed. "Sheriff," she said, "I think you're taking this matter much too lightly. I agree with the children. There is a missing will; there has been skulduggery; and I for one am going to keep a watchful eye on certain people; and shall continue to look for that missing will, though I have just about run out of looking places."

——XII——

The next day was Saturday, and a very subdued Relee knocked on Emma Louise's door. "It's as we thought it would be," he told her glumly, when she answered, "they don't believe us."

"I know," Emma Louise agreed. "It's just hopeless I guess."

"Miss Amanda is still going to look for the desk," Relee said.

"They won't believe it's Gamma's desk even if we find it." Emma Louise would not be cheered.

"I know," hope had gone from Relee's voice. "Last night I asked Dad to help us locate the will at the courthouse so we could compare it with those papers of your great-great-grandfather's. He said even if the signatures were different that wouldn't prove anything after all these years because someone could have

104

planted those papers in the trunk in your attic."

"Well, I never," Emma Louise exclaimed indignantly. "Your dad is the same as saying my family, not the Harrises, are the cheats."

"Not really," Relee said soothingly, "I don't think he takes it seriously. He thinks we're just playing a game. He thinks what Seth did had nothing to do with what we've been doing."

"We almost get killed, and they think we're playing games. The sheriff will probably even turn Seth loose."

"He already has, but I think the Harrises are pretty mad at Seth. Maybe they'll make him leave town."

They sat silently on the steps, each deep in thought. "There's only one thing left to do," Relee said, breaking the long silence. "We've got to dig up your great-great-grandfather's bones and take them to a chemist."

Emma Louise stared at him wide-eyed. "You're kidding."

"No, I'm not. If we can prove he was poisoned they would believe us. I'll bet Gamma will help. What did she have to say about yesterday? We owe her a lot of thanks for saving our lives."

"She didn't come last night. At least, I don't think she did, but I was so tired I went to sleep almost before I got in bed."

"She'll come tonight," Relee said confidently, "and when she does, ask her about digging up the bones. She'll say that's what we have to do. Wait and see."

As Relee predicted Gamma did appear that night. She brushed away Emma Louise's thanks with an airy wave of her hand. "Sorry I didn't run those young rascals away from the woods and over the bluff. 'Twould be good riddance."

"The weird thing, Gamma, is that no one believes they really meant to hurt us. They think it was a prank."

"A prank, indeed," sniffed Gamma. "Blood will tell. Murder runs in that family."

"How did you know we were out there?" Emma Louise asked.

"I heard your mother call the sheriff to report you missing. Later he called her back, and I heard some mention of Lonesome Bluff. It was Lonesome Bluff in my day, and that is one place that hasn't changed. Naturally I went right out to see what was going on. Got there in the nick of time I'd say. We are going to have to be more cautious in our activities."

"They didn't believe us, you know. They don't believe you are real or that the will was forged or that there is a desk or anything." Emma Louise sounded very discouraged.

But Gamma didn't seem the least chagrined. "You didn't expect anything else, did you?" she asked. "I told you we would have to attend to this business ourselves."

"Relee doesn't think finding the will, will do any good. His Dad says they will say that great-great-grandfather's papers were forged."

For once Gamma seemed crestfallen.

"Relee thinks we should dig up great-great-grandfather's bones and take them to a chemist. He thinks they'll find arsenic in the bones or nails or something."

"No doubt they would, but gravedigging is no work for you two." Gamma rocked silently. "Well, I shall have to cudgel my brain about this, so enough talk for tonight," she said at last. "Anyway you need your rest after your experience of yesterday."

Then she was gone.

Emma Louise could not sleep. All that had happened kept turning over and over in her mind. If only she could find the desk, people would have to believe some of her story. And then suddenly as if a bright light had been turned on, she knew where the desk must be. Miss Edwards' house! She had loved old things and had never gotten rid of anything. She had been friends with Faith. Maybe Faith had been so scared when her father married Hettie Harris that she had gotten the desk out of the house for safekeeping. What better place than with her friend Amity Edwards? Then Faith had died young, before she could do anything about the secret.

Feeling strangely certain of the whereabouts of the desk, Emma Louise made plans. She and Relee would go to the Edwards house in the morning right after church. She didn't know how they would get in, just that they would.

In the morning Emma Louise called Relee, and after church met him at the Edwards house. Although in a busy part of town, the house looked lonely and forlorn, its curtainless windows staring at the world like sorrowful eyes. As they opened the creaking gate and walked up the sidewalk that was buckling from the pressure of tree roots, Emma Louise whispered, "It makes me feel funny inside. Like I want to cry, but I don't know why."

"I don't know why either," Relee said. "Why should it make you want to cry? It's just an empty old house."

"Maybe that's why," Emma Louise was still whispering. "It feels so lonely. People used to be happy here, laughing and playing and shouting. It misses all that."

Relee looked at her disgustedly. "Aw, cut that out," he said. "Houses don't feel. You know that."

"No, I don't know that," Emma Louise retorted. "I didn't think there were ghosts, and now I know there are. Maybe ghosts in the house are lonely and looking out through those window eyes."

"I said cut it out. You're giving me the creeps. I thought you wanted to get inside the house instead of standing out here blabbering about ghosts. Just how are we to do it? We can't walk up to the door. Someone might see us."

"It's Sunday. Harris Square is closed, and people can't see the house too well from the other streets because of the fence and trees and bushes."

"OK," Relee agreed. Taking a deep breath, he walked boldly up to the front door. It was locked tight.

"Let's try the windows on the porch," Emma Louise suggested. They, too, were locked.

Relee motioned Emma Louise to follow him around the house. The back and side doors were locked, and they could not reach the windows. However, on one side there was a small opening near the ground almost obscured by an overgrown bush. They squeezed through to find themselves on something like a slide. They had entered the cellar of the old house through the coal shute.

The cellar was dark, cobwebby, and dusty. After their eyes adjusted to the dim light, they were able to make out shadowy shapes. However, except for a few old boxes, an antiquated wash tub, and a rickety chair or two, the cellar was empty.

"This way," Relee urged and led the way to the stairs going up to the house. The door at the top was not locked.

They walked from one high-ceilinged room to another, their footsteps on the bare floor echoing from wall to wall.

"Oh, I like this house," Emma Louise whispered. "Look at the tall windows with the beautiful window seats. And there are fireplaces in every room. Wouldn't you love to live here?"

"No," Relee whispered, "I'll bet it's not even air-conditioned."

"Neither is my house," Emma Louise reminded him. "Anyway, it's dumb of you to think air-conditioning is more important than . . ." She hesitated trying to find the right word to express what she felt, "More important than, well, than beauty."

"What's beautiful about a bunch of empty old rooms?" Relee scoffed.

"If you can't see it, you're just a clod."

"That's gratitude for you," Relee said. "After all I've done for you. I've a good notion to leave right now and forget the whole thing."

"I'm sorry, Relee," Emma Louise apologized. "I shouldn't have said that. People like different things. Please don't go."

"All right," Relee said. "Let's go upstairs. Not

that there's any use looking up there. I don't think there's a stick of furniture in the whole house. Whatever made you think the desk is here?"

"It is here," Emma Louise insisted. "It's got to be. I just know it."

The upstairs was as empty as the downstairs. Relee was soon ready to leave, but one room held Emma Louise's attention. It must have been the children's room, for the fireplace was of beautiful tiles depicting scenes from nursery rhymes.

"Oh, look, Relee," Emma Louise said. "There is the cow that jumped over the moon and Little Bo Peep and Little Boy Blue."

"That's baby stuff," Relee was unimpressed, "come on, let's get out of here."

"Not just yet, Relee," Emma Louise pleaded. "The desk has to be here. I feel it in my bones."

"It is not," Relee said flatly. "We've been everywhere even up to the attic."

"No, wait," Emma Louise said excitedly for she had a sudden thought. "We haven't been everywhere. We couldn't have because we haven't been in a round room."

"What are you talking about?"

"The little tower Miss Amanda calls a turret. We haven't been in anything like that."

"It must be a dummy, not a room at all. We couldn't have missed a room."

But Emma Louise was equally sure that they had. She started running from room to room opening doors and peering into closets. She found nothing but emptiness. Once more they entered the nursery.

"Relee, why can't we find the room?" Emma Louise said in despair. "It has to be somewhere. Do you suppose you get in from the cellar? Or even through a tunnel outside?"

Relee brightened at the mention of tunnel. "Let's try the closet in here, then we'll look in the cellar."

"Nothing here but shelves on the back wall," Emma Louise said and started to close the door.

"No, wait," Relee said as he grabbed the door. "See that leather strap under the middle shelf. Sometimes old doors are opened that way. Help me pull." Together they tugged at the narrow strip of leather.

"Oh, it's moving," Emma Louise shouted. "The whole wall is coming out." Creaking as if it had not moved in years, the shelf-covered door opened.

Through this door Emma Louise and Relee entered a round room that looked as if time had not touched it. An old picture book lay open at what must have been a favorite story. There was a Noah's Ark on the floor with animals lined up beside it as if preparing to enter two by two. A small table was set with tiny plates and cups and saucers. At the table sat a beautiful doll coated with dust. She seemed to be staring at the intruders with an almost startled look on her face. Best of all there was a desk, rather plain and rather dainty.

"There it is," Emma Louise whispered.

"How did you know?" Relee asked wonderingly.

Emma Louise was thoughtful. At last she said, "I don't know for sure, but somehow, someway, someone must have told me."

"Let's turn it upside down and see which leg is hollow," Relee said, starting toward the desk.

Emma Louise held him back. "Wait a minute, I don't think we should touch it. We shouldn't touch anything until we get some grownups here. Maybe when they see that there truly is a desk with a hollow leg and a will, and that it's all covered with dust, they'll believe we aren't making everything up."

"You're right," Relee agreed. "Let's go get my dad, your mom, and the sheriff."

"And Miss Amanda."

"Yes, and Miss Amanda. We'll all come back and read the will." Following Relee down the echoing stairs Emma Louise had a sobering thought.

"Wait," she said, "we may have been followed by Seth and those boys. As soon as we leave they could come in to see what we were looking for."

"Even if they are following us and do get in the house, I bet they'll never find the round room," Relee replied. "No one else did. People emptied the whole house of furniture and they didn't find it. We never would have if you hadn't been so sure and snoopy."

"True, but just the same let's hurry."

——XIII——

But it was hard to hurry. Mr. Grant, relaxed before the television set, was watching his favorite team in a close game. Mrs. Jones wasn't eager either to give up an interesting book she was reading. Miss Amanda, however, was very willing. With a little cajoling and threatening she got the sheriff to agree to go, and it was the sheriff who called Mrs. Jones and Mr. Grant and asked them to meet at the Edwards house. Emma Louise, Relee, and Miss Amanda rode to the house in the sheriff's car. "I'll get a key," the sheriff said on the way. "Ned Murphy, who's foreman of the wrecking crew that's to tear the house down tomorrow will have one. I'll stop by for Archibald Harris, too.

"You can't do that," Relee and Emma Louise protested. "Mr. Harris will never let us in. Look what Seth did to us."

116

"Nonsense," the sheriff said, "you can't judge Harris by his son. Every family has a bad egg now and then."

A somewhat grumpy Archibald Harris followed the sheriff's car to the Edwards house. Emma Louise and Relee led the group through the echoing house up the winding stairway to the nursery. Emma Louise opened first the closet door, and Relee pulled the strap to open the inside door to the round room. Inside they pointed proudly to the dusty desk.

"There it is," said Emma Louise, "and it has a hollow leg with a will inside. I know it does."

The grownups stared around the room in surprise. Archibald Harris had an especially astonished look on his face.

Miss Amanda broke the silence. "I don't believe this room has been touched since Amity Edward's brother died," she said softly. "I've always been told his death was sudden, and the family never got over their grief."

Emma Louise felt tears coming to her eyes. Relee alone seemed unaffected. "Come on," he urged, "let's get the will out of the desk."

"But before we touch it, everyone look," Emma Louise said, "see the dust all around the desk. No one has walked near it in ever so long. Now when you find the will, you'll know that we didn't forge it and put it there."

"Will?" demanded Archibald Harris, "What's this about a will? Sheriff, I thought you said there might be some evidence in this house."

"That's right," the sheriff answered. "A will is evidence. I was told I might expect to find evidence here." He approached the desk slowly, turned it over on it's side, and began to examine the legs. The others clustered closely around.

"Ah," the sheriff said, "see these reinforcements on the bottom of the legs? This one lifts out, and, yes, the leg is hollow." He poked down into it with his pen and pulled out a folded paper. There was complete silence in the dusty room.

Then everyone started talking at once.

"Read it," Relee and Emma Louise cried.

"Can you beat that?" Mr. Grant said. "The kids were right."

"What's this? What's this?" Archibald Harris demanded nervously as the sheriff cleared his throat and began to read the last will and testament of Gamma.

Everything was just as Gamma had said. She had left everything to her daughters. Her husband was to have the use of the property in his lifetime, and then it was to go to Felicity, Patience, Prudence, Faith, Hope, and Charity.

Emma Louise began to jump up and down. "Oh, Mom," she said, "it's true, it's true. We won't be poor anymore. We can loosen our belts and turn up the heat and never be cold again."

"Nonsense," Mr. Harris said, "this will has no meaning. The one down in the courthouse counts. This one could have been planted any time in the last hundred years."

"Maybe so and maybe not," the sheriff cautioned. "At any rate I don't think your wrecking crews should start on this house tomorrow. We have some sorting out to do."

"I fail to see how this in any way affects my plans for this house." Archibald Harris was stiff and curt. "This house has nothing whatsoever to do with this alleged will. And as for the will, my lawyers will make short work of it." With a stiff nod of his head he walked from the room.

"He's right, you know," said the sheriff, "his lawyers can probably get this will thrown out."

"Oh, no," wailed Emma Louise. "It isn't fair."

Emma Louise anxiously awaited Gamma's appearance that night. She waited and waited and waited, but Gamma did not come. "Oh, no," thought Emma Louise, "she knows all is lost, and she has given up hope and gone away forever, and I'll never see her again." Emma Louise climbed into bed, and pulled Gamma's quilt up against her cheeks and cried softly. She couldn't help it. Only after a long while did she sleep.

——XIV——

Someone was shaking her, shaking her rather roughly. Emma Louise opened her eyes to find a soft light brightening the room. Gamma had come back. Overjoyed, Emma Louise sat up quickly and impulsively reached out to hug her, but it was like hugging air.

"Oh, Gamma," Emma Louise said, "I thought you had gone forever. I'm so glad you're here. We found the will, just like you said, but Mr. Harris says that doesn't make any difference. He says his lawyers will take care of that."

"Does he now?" Gamma seemed not in the least perturbed. "We will attend to Mr. Harris. But now there's a more pressing matter. You have to get the sheriff and come to the cemetery right away. They are digging up your great-great-grandfather. I expected something of the sort from that Seth Harris. I have been guarding the grave, and a good thing too. Hurry."

Emma Louise bounded out of bed, not minding the icy floor on her bare feet. She ran straight to her mother's room, turned on the light, and began shaking her mother's shoulder.

"Wake up. Wake up," she urged, "Mom, you've got to wake up and call the sheriff."

Mrs. Jones sat up and looked at her. "Whatever is it now, Emma Louise?" she asked in a sleepy voice.

"Seth Harris and his friends are digging up Great-Great-Grandfather's grave. He was murdered, and his bones will prove it."

"Emma Louise, I don't know where you get these wild notions."

"It's not a wild notion. I was right about the will, wasn't I? Please, Mom," she pleaded, "call the sheriff."

Mrs. Jones started to get out of bed.

"Hurry, hurry," Emma Louise urged, "we haven't a moment to lose."

"Hundred-year-old graves aren't dug up in a matter of minutes," Mrs. Jones said, "if indeed one is being dug up at all. But I will call the sheriff."

"Don't tell him what you want," Emma Louise said. "Just tell him you need him right away. He might not come if you told him about the grave."

"Indeed he might not," Mrs. Jones agreed, "but I shall tell him the truth."

When Mrs. Jones had finished her call, Emma Louise called the Grant house.

"Young lady, do you realize how late it is?" Mr. Grant asked grumpily. "I shall certainly not wake Relee at this hour."

Emma Louise took a deep breath and told Mr. Grant what had happened. He was skeptical, but when she told him the sheriff was on the way to her house, he agreed to come and to bring Relee.

When Emma Louise called Miss Amanda, she did not seem the least bit surprised and agreed to join everyone at Emma Louise's.

And so on that cold, starless night a small procession drove toward the cemetery.

They stopped some way outside, and with the sheriff and Mr. Grant leading, cautiously approached the cemetery ground. The sheriff had stopped by the caretaker's house for the key to the big iron gate. He quietly opened the heavy gate and the group carefully approached the burial plot of Emma Louise's family. The clink of shovels guided them as they came closer, and they were soon near enough to see dark forms digging in the time-hardened earth.

The sheriff's flashlight revealed Seth, Mike, and Ed. Startled, they dropped their shovels and started to run, but in the dark they tripped over the graves and fell. The sheriff and Mr. Grant easily took them in custody.

The next night Emma Louise again waited impatiently for Gamma to appear. She had much to tell. But Gamma did not come that night or the next or the next. Emma Louise was thoroughly worried. The next night, however, Gamma appeared, sitting calmly in her rocker. Without any preliminary greeting, she fixed Emma Louise with her bright eyes and commanded, "Now, child, tell me all about it."

"Oh, Gamma, I'm so glad to see you," Emma Louise cried with relief. "I've waited and waited and been so worried about you. Where have you been?"

"Resting, just resting. There's been too much excitement around here for the likes of me. Been a terrible strain on my powers. But all is well that ends well, and I take it things are ending well?"

"Oh, yes," Emma Louise assured her, "very well. Look, Gamma, look there." And she pointed to the corner of the room opposite Gamma's chair. There, looking very much at home, was the desk.

Gamma stopped rocking and stared thoughtfully at the desk. It almost seemed as if a tear slipped down her cheek. In a moment she said softly, "Lifts the years. Makes it all seem as yesterday." Then she shook her head briskly and said, "Enough of that. I'm glad to see my desk is home at last with my namesake, it's proper owner. Now tell me, child, is my will believed, or are they still talking nonsense about a forgery?"

"Mom and the sheriff and Mr. Grant believe it," Emma Louise assured her. "Mr. Grant says it will be a legal hassle, but we will get everything arranged as it should be. And, oh, Gamma, the best thing happened. Mr. Grant got a court order to stop them tearing down Miss Edward's house because everything the Harrises own has to be frozen while the legal things are untangled. We want to make a museum out of the house with Miss Amanda in charge. Wouldn't Miss Edwards like that?"

"Yes, indeed, I'm sure she would."

"Everything will take a long time I guess," said Emma Louise. "Mr. Harris is still saying the will will be thrown out. Miss Amanda says he is whistling past the graveyard. She thinks he knew all along there was a skeleton in his family closet. You were right, Great-Great-Grand-father was murdered." Saying this made Emma Louise shiver, thinking that it had happened right here in her own house. "They found traces of arsenic. Miss Amanda says some suspicion of what happened must have been passed down in the family. She thinks that's why Seth Harris tried to dig up the body."

"We mustn't be too sure of that," Gamma said. "Don't blame a whole family for the misdeeds of some. I can believe that the present Mr. Harris knew nothing about the murder. His son Seth is probably a throwback to that old Seth. When he heard about murder and a forged will, he naturally believed it for he knew he would have done the same thing in the same circumstances."

Gamma looked slowly about the room. "What are you and your mother's plans, child? Will you fix up the old place or move to fancy new lodgings?"

"Oh, no, we won't move. We'll fix it up, make it warm, and live right here."

"It's a real comfort to know the old place is appreciated, and my namesake will not want for worldly goods. A real comfort. I would say, child, my work is done at last."

The tone of her voice frightened Emma Louise. It sounded quiet and final. Also Gamma seemed to be getting dimmer and dimmer.

"Oh, Gamma," she pleaded, "please stay. Don't go away. You wouldn't go away forever would you?"

"Child, of course I must. I must be about my own business. I'm frightfully overdue."

"Oh, no, no, no. Don't leave. Don't leave." Tears were running in showers down Emma Louise's cheeks.

Gamma rose and came over to the bed. She reached her arms out to hug Emma Louise, but Emma Louise felt nothing but a stir of air.

"Oh, drat it," Gamma said. Once again Emma

Louise thought she saw something like a tear. "This is the one unsatisfactory thing about being a spirit. There's no human warmth in it." She leaned very close to Emma Louise as if to kiss her, but Emma Louise felt only a tiny movement of air as soft as the flutter of a butterfly's wings. She reached out to try to hug Gamma, but the misty image of her was growing even dimmer.

"Take care, child," she heard Gamma saying very faintly. "Mind what I have told you and try to remember your great-great-grandmother Emma Louise.

And then she was gone. Emma Louise was alone. The room was quiet and very empty. Emma Louise lay back on her pillow and pulled Gamma's quilt up under her chin and thought of what she would never know again. Gamma would never again wake her or scold her or tell her secrets or try to hug her. Emma Louise buried her head in her pillow to try to muffle her sobs.

Presently the door opened, and Mrs. Jones came into the room. "Emma Louise," she said in alarm, "whatever is the matter? Are you sick?" She turned on the bedside lamp and reached over to feel Emma Louise's forehead.

"You don't have any fever," she said, relief in her voice. "Why are you crying, dear?"

Emma Louise sat up and threw her arms

around her mother. "Oh, Mom," she said, "She's gone forever, and I'll never see her again."

"Gone? Who is gone, dear?"

"Great-Great-Grandmother. I told you about her. She told me about the will and the desk and Great-Great-Grandfather's being murdered, and everything."

"Yes, dear, I know," her mother said soothingly, "but that's all over now. You really must stop these wild imaginings."

"But I didn't imagine her. She was as real as anything. She was right here in this room. And there is her desk. I didn't imagine that. She told me about it."

"Yes, yes, dear." Mrs. Jones sat holding Emma Louise and stroking her hair. "You have had some strange dreams, but that's all over. Settle down, be happy with our good fortune, and help me make plans."

Emma Louise lay back on her pillow. Her mother tucked the Quilt around her, kissed her softly, turned off the light, and left the room. Emma Louise lay quietly in the darkness that felt very lonely because Gamma was gone.